Lynda

THE MOON WILL

LYNDA E. RUCKER

KAROSHI
BOOKS

The Moon Will Look Strange

First published in the UK by Karōshi Books, an imprint of
Noose and Gibbet Publishing, 2013

Collection in this form copyright © Karōshi Books**, 2013**
All stories copyright © Lynda E. Rucker, 2013
Introduction © Steve Rasnic Tem, 2013

The right of Lynda E. Rucker to be identified as the author of this work has been asserted by her in accordance with the Copyright, Designs & Patents Act 1988.

This is a work of fiction. Names, characters, places and incidents are either the product of the author's imagination or are used fictitiously, and any resemblance to actual persons, living or dead, is entirely coincidental.

All rights reserved. This book is sold subject to the condition that it shall not, by way of trade or otherwise, be lent, re-sold, hired out or otherwise circulated in any form or binding or cover other than in which it is published and without a similar condition including this condition being imposed on the subsequent publisher.

First Paperback Edition

Cover concept: Johnny Mains
Cover design: Andrew Oakes

Published by:
Karōshi Books

ISBN: 978-1492314646

Lynda E. Rucker

PUBLICATION HISTORY

The Burned House - *Original to this collection*
No More A-Roving - DARKNESS RISING #1, 2001
Reprinted 2002 in THE MAMMOTH BOOK OF BEST NEW HORROR, VOLUME 13, edited by Stephen Jones
The Chance Walker - THE THIRD ALTERNATIVE #33, 2003
Available as a podcast, read by Lynda E. Rucker, at Transmissions From Beyond
The Moon Will Look Strange, - BLACK STATIC #16, April 2010
Reprinted in THE YEAR'S BEST DARK FANTASY AND HORROR 2011, edited by Paula Guran
In Death's Other Kingdom - *Original to this collection*
Ash-Mouth - BLACK STATIC #2, December 2007
These Foolish Things - *Original to this collection*
Beneath the Drops - THE THIRD ALTERNATIVE #25, November 2000
These Things We Have Always Known - BLACK STATIC #8, December 2008
Reprinted 2009 in THE MAMMOTH BOOK OF BEST NEW HORROR, VOLUME 20, edited by Stephen Jones
Different Angels - THE THIRD ALTERNATIVE #19, March 1999
The Last Reel - SUPERNATURAL TALES #10, 2006
Reprinted 2007 in THE MAMMOTH BOOK OF BEST NEW HORROR, VOLUME 18, edited by Stephen Jones
Reprinted 2010 in WIELKA KSIEGA HORRORU 1 (Fabryka Słów, Poland)
Podcast October 2012 at *Pseudopod*

The Moon Will Look Strange

Lynda E. Rucker

CONTENTS

INTRODUCTION – STEVE RASNIC TEM
7
AUTHOR'S NOTE
11
THE BURNED HOUSE
15
NO MORE A-ROVING
30
THE CHANCE WALKER
51
THE MOON WILL LOOK STRANGE
74
IN DEATH'S OTHER KINGDOM
92
ASH-MOUTH
111
THESE FOOLISH THINGS
135
BENEATH THE DROPS
139
THESE THINGS WE HAVE ALWAYS KNOWN
160
DIFFERENT ANGELS
177
THE LAST REEL
194
ACKNOWLEDGEMENTS
213

The Moon Will Look Strange

Lynda E. Rucker

INTRODUCTION

Lynda Rucker's first collection *The Moon Will Look Strange* is a good example of why single-author short story collections (and the publishers willing to take them on) are so important to the health and future of fantastic literature. I believe we're currently enjoying a renaissance of finely-written short form fantasy, with numerous new writers appearing every year producing great fiction for both large and small venues. The only downside to this phenomenon is that it's become increasingly difficult to keep up with all the new material.

The majority of these stories first appeared in *The Third Alternative/Black Static*, a magazine I've written for numerous times. Three of the stories were also reprinted in Stephen Jones' *Best New Horror,* and one in Paula Guran's *Year's Best Dark Fantasy*. So I was already familiar with Lynda Rucker's name, and I'd read a couple of her stories and been impressed by them. But there's never enough time for reading new fiction it seems, and (like many avid readers I suspect) I don't read every story in every magazine and anthology I receive, even in the magazines and anthologies I'm in. A writer can toil away for years producing great work for periodicals and anthologies without adequate attention being paid. So Lynda's work wasn't fully on my radar. Thankfully, this collection changes all that. It's startling to discover that the stories reprinted here are her first published stories. So pay attention to Lynda Rucker. I think we can expect great things from her.

I don't believe you can really gauge the significance of a writer until you read a number of their stories at one time. I still remember the sense of delight and discovery I had when I read my first Caitlin R. Kiernan collection. I'm pleased to report that I'm having that same experience after finishing *The Moon Will Look Strange.*

I believe "No More A-Roving" is a kind of keystone for this collection, and emblematic of what she does best. The story is built on a solid foundation of close, realistic character observations. In fact the details are so specific and telling that after a few pages we might think we were reading a piece of realistic contemporary fiction in one of the better literary magazines. But at the right moments we become privy to numerous small, disquieting perceptions. Has he misremembered the name of the hostel and arrived at the wrong place? Why does there seem to be too many sleepers in the dorm? And what is it about that dinghy? In the final analysis some might be inclined to read this as a completely realistic piece, but Lynda Rucker's great talent is that she is able to carefully build a perceptive portrayal of the real world and in the process of that exploration find that edge where the everyday dissolves and the numinous begins. Her compelling execution of this transition strongly echoes the work of Robert Aickman.

The Aickman echoes continue through a number of stories whose settings span the globe. In most of these tales characters are lost, vanished, or disoriented as they struggle to function in realities cobbled together through a compromise between confounding mysteries and a sense of the way things should be. In the post-Kafkaesque world of the Czech Republic, the isolated English instructor of "The Chance Walker" must struggle with a poorly understood language as she deals with memories of her father's suicide while living in an apartment building with too many shadows, too many doors and windows filled in, painted over, or nailed shut. As another character informs her, "this whole country is haunted."

In the Spain of the title story a grieving father seeks oblivion, running away from his wife as he shifts between a desperate need to "vanish off the face of the earth" and his guilt-ridden turmoil over the extreme steps he has undertaken to bring his dead daughter back.

Rucker has a remarkable way with endings. In many of these tales she takes you right up to the peak of rising action, then stops, finally delivering the perfectly calm last few lines which let you know just how badly things have gone wrong. She also has a keen sense of when to release the poetry, so that a story like "Beneath the Drops" (which is also a superior contemporary example of local color writing) skillfully plays with words and images evoking wet versus dry, finally ending in a moving crescendo of language.

The Moon Will Look Strange

Another favorite is "Ash-Mouth," a beautiful rendering of childhood populated with awkward memories, specific books, cherished pets, dreams, and a sister who has gone missing. And yet another is "The Last Reel," with that wonderful description of the isolated house and that delightful stream of movie trivia which almost, but not quite, distracts us from the knowledge that a terrible transference has taken place.

Those are just a few examples, but this is a book full of such fine writing. I eagerly await her next.

Steve Rasnic Tem,
Centennial Colorado,
February 2013

AUTHOR'S NOTE

I was talking to two different people recently about the past, and interestingly, both of them reported the same relationship with it: it doesn't exist for them; it's an utterly inaccessible country. My experience is the opposite. It's nothing to do with nostalgia; it's more that for me, the past is right here with me, all the time. I can summon old conversations at will, I might be able to tell you what we talked about the first time we met even if it was years ago. Time, as such, isn't all that meaningful to me; its passage has always felt arbitrary, moving not at all linearly, rather circling in on itself often as not.

What does all this have to do with the book you're holding in your hands (or reading on your screen) at this very moment? Well, this book is very much a journey into my own past. Some of the stories here were written a very long time ago indeed. And I balked at the first thought of returning to them, reading over them again for this collection. It's an odd thing, looking back at stories you wrote a decade or more ago and finding parts of yourself there, but in the end it was less harrowing than I had imagined it would be. I am pleased to report I still liked all of them. In some cases, they were not the same stories I would write today, or I might have told them somewhat differently—but less so than I would have thought, and they very much still feel like they are *mine.*

And all of them come, in part at least, from a deeply personal place. Settings are important to me, and all of them happen in places that mean a great deal to me, that made impressions on me down to my bones. Memory and place are two preoccupations of mine, although it's not always apparent to anyone who doesn't know where the stories came from. The first reprint in this collection, "No More A-Roving," was the third one published; the landscape of the west of Ireland haunted me for a decade before I put pen to paper to write about it, and I've met nearly all the characters therein on my travels, where I sometimes felt as lost and aimless as the protagonist and those he meets. "The Chance Walker" was born from a stint teaching English in the Czech Republic and a painting of the same name by the Czech artist Jiří Mocek; once upon a time, in a different life, I had a book of his paintings. This one is all about the past, and I, too, once stood on the Polish border looking out at the World War II bunkers feeling unhinged from time.

"The Moon Will Look Strange" was written while staying at the same Albaicín lodging as the story's protagonist, although unlike him, I was so happy there—perhaps the happiest I've ever been in my life—and each day I walked past the wall overlooking the Alhambra that figures in the story. "Ash-Mouth" is, I think, a story of the childhood I wanted when I *was* a child (one who happened to be fascinated with cases of spontaneous combustion): a sister near my age to share my imaginings with.

"Beneath the Drops" oozed from a dismal Pacific Northwest winter in Eugene, Oregon, when I—born and raised in the relentlessly sunny South—started to believe it might never stop raining. "These Things We Have Always Known" began as sentences scrawled on a yellow legal pad, sitting outside in the sunshine on a fifteen minute break from an excruciatingly dull temp job and wishing I could be almost anyplace else, when I began to imagine the weird rituals and requirements of office clerical tasks might take on a much more sinister significance. I was still on the West Coast but feeling homesick, so I located it in the North Georgia mountains where my father grew up and infused it with the small town atmosphere of my own upbringing.

"Different Angels" has part of its genesis in a never-forgotten nightmare from my childhood, the same nightmare Jolie has about the devil tunneling up near the jonquils. The final story in the collection, "The Last Reel," came from yet another childhood nightmare, this one of a witch living at my grandmother's house. I vividly remember elements of the nightmare itself all these years later, and the layout of the house matches the old shotgun she and my grandfather lived in.

The reprints mark, for me, what feels like the end of one era of my writing, perhaps because "The Moon Will Look Strange" serves as a bridge between a stretch of several years in which I took a break from writing for publication and the years since. I spent

The Moon Will Look Strange

that seemingly-fallow time in part working on an MA in medieval English literature and hoping to recalibrate my relationship to writing fiction, which had mostly become a source of frustration and discouragement for me—and writing offers so few external rewards that I feel that if I've lost the joy of the process, there's no point in doing it. The recalibration worked, and the three stories original to this collection are among those that come from the other side of that. Maybe time does exist for me a little bit, because I feel as though I have a lot less perspective on them and the person who wrote them; I lack the luxury of distance.

There are more stories out there now, about memory and place and other things such as ghosts and loss, and there are many more stories to come. But this collection is, in many ways, the story of my origins as a writer, what I remember and where I went and who I was, and they shaped all that has come since.

Lynda E. Rucker
Dublin, Ireland
August 29, 2013

The Burned House

One, you're at the yard . . .

The burned house stood at the back of a scrubby lot. If a house could be said to glower, then glower it did: rising from the ashes which were all that was left of its south face, sitting back on its haunches, its wooden front porch inexplicably wrapped in chicken wire (to keep out trespassers? to keep something in?), its second floor rearing up and threatening to topple.

The *For Sale* sign had been there forever—whoever had first put it there was probably dead by now—and punctuated the scene like a particularly unfunny joke. Nobody was ever going to buy the burned house.

Agnes Swithin, jogging through the chilly dusk, her breath steaming, slowed and then stopped before it. Her kneecap had begun to throb again. She clutched at the splintery fence with hands that looked older than she felt, the skin translucent over knots of prominent blue veins, and willed the pain to move up through her body and out her fingers. The doctor said running made it worse, but Agnes couldn't bear being sedentary. *Why don't you try swimming or walking*, the doctor had said helpfully, a fresh-faced young woman Agnes might have taught just a few years earlier, who clearly (Agnes imagined) thought that she, Agnes, ought to be engaged in a more geriatric form of exercise. Afternoons in the pool at the Y surrounded by soft fleshy women wearing bathing suits modestly trimmed with skirts. Yoga for the ancient and decrepit. Agnes had never actually been to the senior yoga class, the pool, or even the Y itself, but she felt she could picture it all the same.

She caught her breath, then, not from exertion, nor from the pain in her knee.

A girl in a white dress had emerged from round the south side of the house. The girl was thin—too thin, transparently thin, head and hands and feet like bough-breaking burdens on the ends of twiglike neck and arms and legs. The legs were bare, the dress stark white against tanned skin. Or it might have been a nightgown. She could have been twelve, fifteen, older; her frailty lent her an ageless quality. Agnes, who resolutely did not believe in ghosts, imagined for a bad moment or two that she was looking at precisely that.

Two, you're through the gate . . .

The truth about the burned house was that if you thought about it too much, you realized it was an enigma, only nobody thought about it much at all. The house had stood in its dilapidated state for as long as anyone knew, including Agnes, who had just entered her seventh decade. The house had neither been condemned nor selected for restoration; it simply was. Yet over those decades it could not be said to have deteriorated further, not in any significant sense. The roof ought to be gone, the walls collapsed, the house reduced to a pile of boards over its long years of neglect, and it was not. A gutter might have unhinged itself, a pilaster might have crumbled, but overall it aged with an enviable and impossible grace, apparently ticking along in its very own timestream.

People rarely noticed, because they rarely thought about the burned house. Sometimes it was remembered in the manner of a dream that returns moodily and incompletely to consciousness: "Oh! I wonder if the burned house is still there?" Rarely did anyone venture to find out. Just as dreams never make sense as the conscious mind tries to catch hold of them, neither did the burned house.

The lots on either side of it were empty, and an old bungalow sat on the one just behind it, a bungalow perpetually for rent because it never kept its tenants long. A weatherbeaten Big Wheel waited forlornly in the weeds of the neat brick ranch house just across the street.

The dead-end street itself had bad associations: people tended to avoid it, although nobody could really say why. There was little reason to turn down it unless you were unfortunate enough to live there, for however short a time, and if you were tempted to do so—perhaps you had followed confusing and incomplete directions and needed to turn the car around and start over in the opposite direction—well, there was a more agreeable cul-desac a block away that would do. Agnes rarely if ever had gone for a run down the street on which the burned house stood. Earlier, as the evening was creeping in, she had been on the phone with her brother, and something he said stirred old memories, and she thought as others had done before her—*oh! the burned house!*—and now she was here, just before the gate, like the old jump rope rhyme they'd recited as children.

Three, you're at the window . . .

The girl raised an arm in greeting, and Agnes raised one back, reassured. It seemed unlikely that a ghost would proffer a friendly hello.

The girl said, "You look cold. Why don't you come in and have some coffee?"

Her voice was not ghostly, either; in fact, a south Georgia twang flattened it, same as most everyone in those parts. She pronounced coffee "cawfee." Agnes, whose curiosity had nearly been her undoing on more than one occasion, said that did sound tempting.

"Come on round the back," said the girl.

Agnes said, "No, I couldn't, really," or maybe it was, "No, I *shouldn't*"; or she intended to. Yet even as she thought to say it she picked her way through the knee-high weeds of the front yard, and heard herself not declining the invitation, but describing the scene to an acquaintance later: *It was like some unseen force had taken hold of me.* That didn't seem quite right. If an unseen force had you in its grip, would you necessarily know what it did or did not compel you to do? Would it move you bodily, or would it nestle in the folds of your brain, induce you to actions even as you continued to believe that you were in charge of yourself? She thought this even as she rounded the corner to a backyard more overgrown than the front, as she observed the broken windows, the scattering of dead leaves across the concrete steps of the back porch, even as she knew when the girl took her hand that she took the hand of a ghost.

Four, you're tempting fate . . .

More than fifty years ago, as children, Agnes and her brother and their friends had dared one another to go near the burned house—to pass through its wooden gate, to run and touch its crumbling chicken-wire porch—but Agnes, at least, never got that close. Her brother, an important (by his account) Los Angeles entertainment attorney, had not returned to town since their mother's untimely death from breast cancer thirty years earlier. *Don't know how you do it, Aggie*, he would say with false heartiness over the phone. He never said what he meant by "do it"; staying in one place, she supposed, years of teaching science at the local high school. Her life must have seemed impossibly dull to him.

I dare you; I double dare you; I double double dare you; I double triple dare you! With such linguistic improbabilities they raised the stakes so high that somebody had to give sooner or later. They'd conjured shapes at the window of the burned house, and shadows of the dead lurching through the ash. And when they jumped rope or played hopscotch or wanted to scare their smaller siblings, they had the jump rope rhyme. Agnes could no longer remember all the words but it was a piece of silly counting doggerel. The words and cadence kept her awake as a child as she invented superstitions to accompany them; if she spoke without errors, she could pass another night safely.

Five, you're past the doorway . . .

"Coffee," the girl said again, as if to remind her.

The kitchen was an old-fashioned one, which only made sense, Agnes supposed. The neat gas stove with its quaint cupboard-sized oven bore the name "Magic Chef" in script-like letters. In the corner stood an icebox, its wooden doors fixed shut with heavy metal clasps. The room stirred a memory of her grandmother's kitchen. But a fine undisturbed ash covered the countertops, the range, the large wooden table flush against the far window, the chairs and the sink. Agnes trailed one finger through the cinders along the counter nearest her. When she looked again at the mark she'd left it was gone. *As if I am the ghost, not her.*

The girl thrust a steaming cup of not-ghostly

coffee at her. "Milk? Sugar?"

"Black," said Agnes. She sipped. The coffee tasted eighty years old.

The girl was not drinking any coffee herself. The house was as cold inside as it was outside, but the girl looked flushed. As Agnes watched, little blisters appeared on her upper lip, then the bare skin of her arms, and then, as her lips blackened, she said, "I'm sorry," and fled through the adjoining blue door.

Agnes waited, but the girl did not reappear. She put down the mug of coffee and followed the girl through the door.

Six, you're in the hall . . .

Agnes and her brother were not, had never been, close. They did not reminisce fondly about the past. On the rare occasions that they did speak, they talked about nothing: his latest wife, the antics of his spoiled children, which of his hot new clients she might have heard of. (None—he did a lot of work for West Coast hip hop artists, whose names Agnes only recognized through the occasional overheard student conversation.) They never really discussed Agnes's life, and they both preferred it that way; he didn't like to listen and she didn't like to share.

But earlier that evening she'd phoned because she thought she remembered that one of her nieces had a birthday coming up soon. She had a vague, unrequited sense of obligation toward the lot of them, although she had trouble keeping names and numbers

The Moon Will Look Strange

straight (having never met them, for one thing). And it turned out she had just missed Cameron's birthday—a nephew, not a niece—and he was out, anyway, so that left Agnes and her brother exchanging uncomfortable pleasantries.

Her brother was the one who brought it up. "The damndest thing," he said. "One of my client's houses almost burned down the other night, and it got me thinking about that burned house, the one we used to play in. You remember it?"

She remembered it, but they never went inside; she was sure of it.

"No," he said, "no, I did. You weren't there, maybe. I remember I was with some older kids."

She asked what it was like.

He barked out a little laugh. "Scary as hell," he said. "I wonder if kids still play around it. Kids there still play outside anymore? They don't here."

"I can't imagine it's still there any longer," she said, even though she knew better.

"Maybe not." He sounded regretful.

"How's Veronica?" she said. Veronica was his new wife. He told her, but she wasn't listening anymore. He'd unlocked the jump rope chant in her head, at least a few lines of it, and those lines kept running circles till they ran her right down to the burned house itself.

Seven, on the stairway . . .

No one waited in the hallway beyond. No footsteps, no sounds of life at all. For one moment Agnes thought it was snowing inside; then she realized it was fine cinders, swirling and falling all about her. Her footprints vanished as made them, buried by the ash.

Framed photographs hung along the wall, covered in blackened, melting glass. She wondered then where the light source lay; it could only be glowing embers of the fire itself, but she saw no actual flames. Agnes passed several closed doors on her way to the staircase at the front of the house. She knew that stairs in a derelict house were likely to be dangerous, but she couldn't bring herself to leave after having seen so little. All along the stair runner, a blue carpet woven with gold threads, little burning rings formed and re-formed. She was sorry she hadn't asked the girl her name, so she could call for her.

Top of the stairs, and another corridor. She followed the crackling sound, and the smell of smoke.

Behind her, a child's voice said, "Hello."

The small boy was dressed in blue striped pajamas.

"Have you come to rescue us?" the boy asked.

Eight, you feel the pall . . .

"No," Agnes's mother had said. "No, I don't want you playing around that old place. Wasn't it condemned?" It was not.

The Moon Will Look Strange

"What happened?" Agnes asked her mother. "Do you remember? Who lived there? Did anybody die when it burned?" She was so young that she still believed herself immortal, and thought those capable of dying a different species altogether.

"Oh, it's a terrible story. They couldn't get the children out in time. Some people said it was the mother, that she'd drugged the household so she could run away with a man that night." Her mother paused significantly. "A Negro man," she said. "It happened in the evening, just before nightfall. The husband was out of town on business. Some people said those children weren't even his." Her mother kissed the top of her head. "You shouldn't think about it, Agnes Swithin. It happened a long time ago, before you were born. Even I was just a baby. Who's been filling your head with stories?"

Agnes, wondering who the children could belong to if not their father, said, "No one."

Nine, you're walking slowly . . .

Agnes could not say why she felt some time had passed, but she was certain of it. She looked at her watch, the expensive Garmin she'd bought to train for a 10K before the knee injury, but its face had melted.

"I don't know. Do you need rescuing?"
"My sister says so. Where is she?"

"I don't know," Agnes said. "She asked me and then . . . " She had almost said *she vanished*, but it seemed rude; was it wrong to remind a ghost that it was, in fact, a ghost?

The boy said, matter-of-factly, "No one ever helps us."

Agnes wondered what kind of help she could possibly render. To the south, the corridor was lost in darkness. The burned wing. "What's down there?"

The boy, who had come to stand beside her, replied in the same matter-of-fact voice. "That's where we died."

They walked toward it together. Agnes had begun to shiver with the cold, but as they neared the south wing, although she could still see nothing, she felt the heat of the flames. She hoped the boy would not begin to blacken and char beside her as the girl had done downstairs.

He came to an abrupt stop long before she could see the corridor's end. He said, "You're not a kid." She didn't answer, and he added, "I can't keep going."

But Agnes could. She remembered as she walked that the burned wing was nothing but ash now, and wondered what she must look like to an observer: two stories high and floating on air.

Ten, watch where you tread . . .

The Moon Will Look Strange

The child's game said you were "getting warmer" as you approached the source. Agnes never saw the burned south wing until she was in it. One moment the corridor lay dark before her; the next, she stepped into the flames.

Agnes gasped. She walked on flames; they could not touch her but they billowed out before her like a grand cascading carpet. The fire roared in her ears, and beyond that lay only silence. The smoke rose about her but she did not breathe it. She reached out to touch a doorknob licked by fire, and passed her hand through the flames without injury.

The door swung open at her touch. She passed through another doorway, where the room was engulfed, as was the four-poster bed in the center. As she drew nearer, she saw the boy and his sister there, looking for all the world as though they slept peacefully.

The boy's eyes snapped open. "You're not a kid," he said again. "It's only kids who can come here. Why are you here? Who are you? What's wrong with you?" His face had turned dark, and angry.

Agnes tried to speak, to tell them something, but when she opened her mouth, smoke wafted out instead of words.

Eleven, bid goodbye now . . .

Agnes is ten years old. Someone has just told her that after you're dead, your nails and hair keep growing. For some reason, Agnes has understood this to mean that if she removes her nails and hair, she will never, ever die. She trims her nails too close to the quick but cannot yet bring herself to go any further; she has already chopped her hair close against her scalp when her mother comes across her sobbing at her reflection in the bathroom mirror. Later her mother will take her for her first-ever hair appointment at a beauty shop downtown, where a girl will valiantly try and fail to make sense of the butchery Agnes has inflicted upon her own locks.

Agnes is sixty-one years old. Someone has just told her it's always cold where the dead sleep, even the dead who have burned to death. Who would tell her such a thing? Maybe it was a thing she dreamed. In this gloaming, in this dying of the day, the burned house is burning down and the dead are dying all the time. Soon, dying is all the dead know how to do. But this time is different. And time is different here. This time is sirens; someone has seen the flames leaping from the burned house, and called the emergency numbers. But the fire will be fought from the outside. No one will risk themselves racing into the burned house, because they imagine there will be no one inside to save.

Twelve, you're here instead . . .

The Moon Will Look Strange

"One thing," said her brother. They had said their goodbyes already. Agnes had one hand on the front doorknob; she was ready to drop the phone on the counter and head out on her run. "One thing," he said again. "Don't go near the burned house. Or the place where it used to be, at least."

Agnes said, "Why on earth would I do that?"

"Just don't."

Thirteen, now you're dead . . .

Agnes Swithin dreams in flames. Yellows, oranges blues and reds, blazing, writhing, birthing sparks that flare into new and bigger fires, blackened wood and charred flesh and all transformed, gone to cinder, gone to ash.

She can see shapes of people gathering, lining the sidewalk outside. She will run to them. She is a good runner, and she will join them easily. She leaps to her feet, but something is holding her back. They have her by the arms, the girl and her brother, and when she looks at them their faces are not the smooth unblemished faces of childhood, but burned and ravaged horrors. Surely she can shake them free; she will tear their arms from their sockets if she has to. She staggers forth and she can hear the murmur going up from the crowd. "Someone's in the fire."

She tries to call out to them, to tell them yes, someone *is* in the fire, it's Agnes Swithin, the biology teacher from the high school. They will know her. They will save her. She can even see some of their faces, some she recognizes: students, and parents of students, some of whom she taught as well. And yet the two are still tugging at her, and all of them are weeping. A large burning chunk of the second story roof plummets before her, throwing up more flames and black, choking smoke and cutting off the rest of the world. The faces, the crowd itself, are lost to her now. Now she clutches the hands that restrain her. They are all she has, and she holds on tight. They whisper as they draw her deeper, telling of a house with a thousand and more rooms, of corridors you could walk forever and a day, telling of things born of fire, born of infernos, born of boredom, born of loss. The house is still burning, they are passing into secret and febrile places, and outside the burned and burning house, the late winter dusk is falling, falling into night.

No More A-Roving

The Seagull Hostel wasn't mentioned in Paul's battered copy of *Let's Go*, but the Australians he'd drunk with back in Cork had recommended it to him, as had his last lift across the Dingle Peninsula. Now dusk had come and gone and a good Irish mile or two out from town he'd begun to wonder if he hadn't been misled. The wind and the chill rain had redoubled their efforts against him, and the couple of cars out on the roads had flown past him in a spray of water. The backpack had seemed so light the first time he'd packed and hefted it. Now it sat like a ton of bricks across his shoulders and lower back. Perhaps he should hike back into town, before it got too late, and blow his budget on some cramped, overpriced bed and breakfast; but there it was, after all, a signpost pointing him down a muddy lane to a rambling wooden structure. In the dark of the night it was merely an outline. It looked deserted.

Paul swore under his breath as he approached it, but just as he was stepping up onto the porch the door swung open before him. "Come in, love, you'll catch your death," and the dumpy middle-aged woman was pulling him in out of the elements. Paul's eyes took a few minutes to adjust to the room before him: hostel-sparse and dingy, a few old chairs and a black and white television in one corner playing the theme to a soap opera, sunny Australian voices ringing incongruously across the gloom.

"Awful night for it," the woman commented needlessly. "Lucky you weren't knocked down by a car with no moon out there. Will you be wanting your own room or a bed in the dormitory, then?"

"Dorm," he said. He'd get a night's sleep and head out in the morning. The Seagull, he realized now that he'd finally found it, was too far from town to suit him. Even a trip to the pub would require him to slog back through that endless wet rainy night. Hadn't the Australians described it as being closer in? Perhaps the name hadn't been the Seagull at all, perhaps the Seabreeze or the Seaview. He might have missed his intended destination entirely in the storm. All the same he might find someone interesting to talk to here, even a travelling companion.

"Right, dear. Six pound fifty. I'm Mrs. Ryan and my girl Laura works from time to time too. Kitchen's through that door there." She pointed. "We don't lock you out during the day, but we ask that if you'll be staying you'll let us know by noon."

Wandering past her, down a short passageway and into the kitchen, he saw why he'd thought the place deserted. All the lit rooms were here at the back. Two girls sat giggling at a rough wooden table in the bare narrow room, spooning yogurt from tiny Yoplait containers. Paul lowered his backpack gratefully to the floor. He nodded at them and they giggled in return.

"I'm Paul," he said, "what's your names?"

They were from Cork, they told him, come here for work. Day in, day out, they gutted fish at one of the warehouses. Seventeen years old and their faces were hard and flat, their accents so thick he had trouble understanding them. Their complacency depressed him. When he wasn't directly addressing them, they whispered to one another and giggled more. At what, he wondered; his relentless American desire to strike up a friendly conversation? In the last year he had learned that things about himself which he had long imagined to be the very essence of Paulness were in fact culturally concocted mannerisms. The discovery was troubling, as though something vital had been stolen from him.

At last he got to his feet and retrieved his backpack, meaning to retreat to the dormitory. If no one there proved worth talking to either, at least he could read for a while before he went to sleep. Reading would distract him from thoughts of Alyssa; she'd stood him up in Scotland where they'd planned to catch the ferry to Ireland together. He'd even stayed two extra days in Stranraer, dull port town, waiting for her to arrive. Somehow, her behavior, though unexpected, hadn't surprised him. Presumably she'd gone on ahead of him, was most likely somewhere in Ireland still. Had he been Alyssa, he wasn't entirely certain he'd have waited on himself either; the real surprise was that she'd not ditched him earlier. And now he'd been travelling so long he found himself running out of reasons not to go home.

The dormitory was at the end of the hallway, past some doors he assumed were private rooms. Stocked with eight bunk beds, it was deserted save for a large young man snoring atop one. The bare walls and windows threw the harsh overhead light back at him. A door at the other end, open slightly to the outside, concealed the couple on the other side of it, a male and female speaking something that sounded like German, or maybe it was Dutch. The scent of hashish drifted languorously across the room.

Paul chose the bed farthest from the snorer to dump his pack. Something he'd seen earlier, in the reception room, worried at the back of his mind. Something he'd noticed, and he couldn't put a name to it.

He was too tired, and exhaustion was playing tricks on him.

He backtracked to the bathroom, a cavernous cold place, to change into dry clothes for sleeping, and brushed his teeth under a bulb that made his face look sickly and orange. So complete was the quiet and sense of isolation that he jumped when the door swung inward and a yellow-haired boy strode past to the urinal.

Paul heard voices in the passageway as he gathered up his shaving kit. They were still hanging around outside the dormitory room when he stepped into the hallway. Four of them, two girls and two younger-looking guys, their voices loud and edgy and frayed by alcohol and cigarettes. Paul found that all at once he didn't feel sociable any longer. Another moment and they were joined by the yellow-haired boy. Paul pushed past them and they gave him the indifferent glances of a well-established travelers' clique.

Another body had occupied the lower bunk opposite Paul's, a small form entirely hidden under the comforter save for some ginger curls strewn across the pillows. Paul rummaged in his backpack

The Moon Will Look Strange

for one of the paperbacks he'd picked up in Dublin.

But the book bored him. He let it slide to the floor and rolled over, shutting his eyes against the glaring light overhead. He thought of home; it was like swallowing bile. Things would look better in the morning. As sleep overtook him, the something unremembered worried at the edges of his mind. Something he'd seen when he first came in, and only now had begun to realize the significance of. Sleep claimed him before he could sort it out.

*

He was awakened by the sound of a child crying. He opened his eyes to a room gone dark, and lifted his head before he realized the sound was that of the wind. He got up quietly, taking care not to irritate the vocal springs of the sagging bunk bed as the slow breath of sleepers rose and fell around him. There seemed too many of them, from the sound of it; only eight bunk beds and not all of them filled, but so many different breaths. A recollection of waking earlier, too, stirred in him, a memory of someone clambering onto the top bunk above him, but the bunk was empty, its bedding smooth. Stealing over to the window Paul saw that the rain had stopped and the sky partially cleared; the wind blew heavy, fast-moving clouds across a moonlit sky. Under the sound of the wind the sea crashed, closer to the hostel than he'd realized. His own breathing fell into a rhythm with it. His eyes adjusted—indeed, the sea lay just beyond, moonlight glinting off the water. Paul leaned closer, pressed his face against the glass as if that might aid his vision. Surely he imagined the tiny boat on the water, manned by several figures, mere silhouettes in the moonlight. A rowboat. And somewhere out to sea, a distant glow, as if a lighthouse on some long-deserted island kept its covenant to beam would-be sailors to safety. Yet no one would dare that cold wild sea, even in daylight, in such a craft. A second possibility occurred to him: perhaps they were in trouble, perhaps there'd been some accident at sea and their vessel had sunk, and Paul was the only person in the world who could rescue them now. His gaze roamed wildly round the room as though he might find help there, wishing he'd never awakened, wishing someone else had spied the boat. He must have mistaken some trick of the moonlight. He would have to go outside, get closer, to be certain.

He felt his way along the wall till he found the door that had sat ajar earlier in the evening. He pulled hard on it, but it did not budge. Paul ran a hand over the knob, looking for some lock to be twisted, and above it in search of a deadbolt. Nothing. The surface of the knob and door were utterly smooth, yet as he tugged on the handle he felt not the slightest *give*.

Panic settled over him like a dream. Back to the window. He must alert someone. But who? Would he wake someone in the room, race to the reception telephone and phone the local police?

But he no longer spied the boat. A trick of light, indeed. He scanned the surface of the water, uncertain of what he was looking for. Sometimes, when he was very tired, dreams lingered like after images. Surely that had happened tonight.

The Moon Will Look Strange

The stillness closed round him again. Something in the hostel was not waiting, not waiting for anything at all. He returned to his bed where sleep came much later, and troubled.

*

The next sound that awoke him was that of the heavy boy gasping his way through a round of calisthenics. In the harsher morning light—for the day dawned like slate—he saw that the boy was more of a man, at least in his late twenties or early thirties. The boy-man wore the clothes of someone even older, clothes Paul associated with the middle-aged or elderly—white undershirt, boxers, black socks pulled up to his knees. The man was trying to touch his toes. He bent at the waist and bobbed up and down. Paul closed his eyes again. His watching might be intrusive. When he opened them again, the man stood over him, sweating.

"Name's David," he said, sticking out a fat, sweaty palm for Paul to handle. "Welcome to the Seagull. Did you just come from Dublin?" He was English.

"Paul," Paul said, though he didn't offer his own hand in return.

David remained undaunted. "On holiday, are you? From America?"

Paul looked past him for the group from the previous night, or the German couple. But he and David were alone. It must be later than he realized. He was very tired. He'd been travelling so much lately. It might be good to stay another day or two and rest.

"Never really had any interest in going to America," David said. "Like it here." He depressed Paul in some unaccountable way. "You at university?"

"Yes," Paul said. He started to offer more, but offering more led to conversation. Paul did not want to converse with David.

When he was able to escape, he located Mrs. Ryan and told her he'd be staying another night. He was shocked to see by the clock behind her that it was almost noon. Mrs. Ryan looked irritated, as if in waiting she'd had to turn away a bevy of travelers clamoring for his bed.

He showered and took a walk out the back of the hostel and down near the water. He found the coastline here forbidding. The green treeless landscape led right up to the edge of the sea, a sheer drop; to the south climbed a rocky cliff. Cold sea spray stung his face. He thought he saw two figures through the fog, clambering up the cliff. Perhaps the German girl and her boyfriend. He shouted after them. After all, they were staying there together, and it was perfectly permissible, expected, even, to strike up a conversation under such circumstances. But they either ignored him or didn't hear, though the girl did turn once and stare at him, hair whipping about her face, before turning back to follow her boyfriend further up and out of sight.

The beacon he recalled from the night before managed to penetrate the mist with a soft yellow glow. A lighthouse, perhaps, on some rocky, craggy island off the coast here? He would ask Mrs. Ryan

The Moon Will Look Strange

about it later. If the light he'd seen was real, had the boat been as well? The dinghy caught his eye, then, drawn up to the shore below though he could see no way of getting down to it. Seeing it there surprised him; he'd have imagined that at some point high tide would obliterate the narrow stretch of beach, making it a gamble to leave anything there. And the choppy sea seemed hardly an ideal waterway for the poor craft. Paul shivered against the chill, and in the next moment recalled his dream of the night before. And certainly it had been a dream. Otherwise, the people he'd seen in the boat had been lost at sea, their tiny boat washed ashore. And it would have been his fault. He tried to imagine it, adrift on that icy ocean, perhaps for days; perhaps worried that to come too close to the rocky cliffs dotting the shorelines there would break the boat up entirely, smash it against the rocks.

His imagination was getting away from him again.

Later today he'd trek into town and pick up a few things to eat and see about bus connections to Tralee and Limerick, anyplace east of here. He'd had enough of the countryside, enough of the coast, and this was seeming less like a restful waystation and more like a place where weary travelers went to die. Something crawled down his spine at the thought, surprising him. *Something just walked over my grave.* Paul stuffed his hands in his pockets and turned his back to the sea, but the chill still stung at the tips of his ears, the back of his neck, needling his skin.

*

"That's Alyssa's scarf!"

Paul didn't think he'd meant to speak out loud. He'd been watching television in the lobby, wrapped in his jacket against the chill he hadn't noticed when he arrived the night before. But the thing that had bothered him the previous night dawned on him now; it was the soft grey woolen muffler snug against Mrs. Ryan's throat. How many times had he seen Alyssa wrap it round her own beautiful neck?

"What, love?" Mrs. Ryan, propped before a tiny space heater with a magazine, looked over at him.

Paul recognized it as though it were a beloved article of clothing belonging to him, the black threads woven throughout the grey in a checkered pattern, the edges frayed because the scarf was old and Alyssa had loved it too much to throw it out.

"Did someone leave that here?" he asked. "The scarf, I mean?"

Mrs. Ryan looked confused. "My scarf?"

"Yes, I think it belongs to a friend of mine." Impatient. Alyssa might be somewhere close by. She might have left only just before he arrived. She might have said where she was going. What he would say to her if he caught up to her, he would not think about.

"Why, no, that's impossible. My husband, God rest his soul, gave me this one Christmas—oh, six, seven years gone now it is. Keeps me warm as can be."

The Moon Will Look Strange

"Did a girl named Alyssa stay here in the last week or so?" Paul demanded. Angry now, he tried to control his tone. She was lying. "It's—I need to get in touch with her. It's very important to me to know if she's been here."

"You're the first new guest I've had in a while," Mrs. Ryan told him placidly. He could hardly accuse her of anything, could he? He could hardly tell her outright that he knew she was a liar. Paul's hands curled into fists and he shoved them deep in jacket pockets. Cheap old bitch. Wouldn't heat the place properly and stole from the guests. And he hadn't made it into town to check on bus connections after all. Well, tomorrow, he'd just leave. He'd get up early and go and sometime during the day he was bound to catch either a bus or a lift out of town.

Paul pushed himself up from the chair and without another word to Mrs. Ryan stalked down the hallway to the dormitory. The group he'd encountered the night before were apparently out again, as was the German couple. The form on the bed opposite his was still there, but this time the covers were thrown back to reveal a small face beneath the ringlets. Paul noticed a bottle of vodka peeking out from the girl's backpack.

Perhaps he'd try walking into town now. The night had cleared, and it wouldn't be such a bad walk as long as it stayed that way. He might even talk to someone about bus schedules. He asked David about a good pub.

"Try O'Flaherty's," David suggested, and Paul realized with a sort of horror that David was preparing to accompany him. The thought of the pub immediately lost its appeal, and he began fumbling over excuses as to why he wasn't really interested in going *tonight*, especially. David, undaunted, took off for town, wearing a heavy overcoat and good boots. Soon after Paul began to wish he'd accompanied him after all. He had no wish to return to the reception room to watch television with Mrs. Ryan, and the German couple returned but spoke in low voices with one another. Paul didn't remember falling asleep atop his covers with all his clothes on, and he didn't wake again before morning.

*

The rain started again soon after he got up, and he couldn't see heading out to hitchhike or wait for a bus in that weather. Anyway, he'd overslept again.

He boiled instant coffee in a deserted kitchen and later made his way out back again to the sea. He looked for his fellow travelers again, perhaps on the cliffs, but saw no one. He smoked the cigarettes he'd bummed from David and threw the butts into the ocean. A bitter wind blew across the water, and somewhere through the mist the beacon shined for someone. He thought of the fishermen who made their living from this sea, of the thousands upon thousands dead of blighted potatoes, years of famine scarring this green harsh land, and he thought of America. The more he thought of it the more it seemed to him to exist someplace very far away. He wondered if he crossed this sea if it would be there any longer. He wondered if he cared.

The Moon Will Look Strange

He strode to the edge, where he'd seen the dinghy below. The strip of shoreline remained, but the dinghy was gone.

It crossed his mind that perhaps it had broken free from its moorings somewhere, drifted up on the tide here and then back out again, but that hardly seemed likely. There had been a deliberateness about its placing on the shore below, as though someone had pulled it in from the water and carefully placed the oars crossways inside of it.

He asked Mrs. Ryan about it that night in the reception room, but she shook her head. "Oh, love, it might be anybody's. Still some fishermen in these parts, you know. We're not all in the business of providing warm beds for tourists." But who would row a dinghy on that wild sea? And there were no lighthouses off shore around here, she assured him, she was certain of that. As she spoke Paul couldn't keep his eyes off that muffler round her neck. He was wild to get hold of it. He'd remembered how to be sure: something he'd teased Alyssa about. She'd written her name on the tags of all her clothes like a child going away to summer camp: Alyssa Meiers. It was an oddly homey and endearing move from the usually elusive, too-beautiful-to-be-true girl. Not the kind of girl who usually fell for Paul. Not the kind of girl he could expect to wait for him to catch up now. And the two of them, together, would have always been that way: Alyssa, far ahead, and Paul, lagging behind, trying to reach her.

In the kitchen he cooked up some packaged noodles and ate them in front of the television. The ginger-haired girl made an appearance outside of her bed at last. She said her name was Rosie and she was from Melbourne. He wondered why she kept getting up and leaving the room until he realized she was refilling her Pepsi can with alcohol. Her speech became slurred and she stumbled once across the rug at the threshold, and she tried to laugh it off but she looked like she was crying. Then she left the room again and didn't come back. Paul was glad. He waited until he was pretty sure she'd gone to sleep, or passed out, and made his way in there as well.

In the morning another girl kneeling beside Rosie, trying to wake her, roused him from sleep instead. "Ah, Rosie, did you have too much to drink again?" the girl was saying, her voice a pleasing Irish cadence, and Paul caught sight of Rosie's face, screwed up tight against the morning like a little girl's, fists rubbing shut eyes. He rolled over and tried to sleep again.

But, "I don't want to go," Rosie whined, "the others have gone and I don't want to go after them."

"There, shhh," the Irish girl whispered as though she were soothing a small child. "No need to fret about it." Later, Paul found the girl in the reception area. This was Mrs. Ryan's Laura, then. She was checking in the first new guest Paul had seen since he arrived, a tall, heavy-set blonde girl.

"Did a girl named Alyssa Meiers stay here before I came?" Paul asked Laura, hoping she'd be more receptive than her mother.

"Oh, I'm sure she didn't. I've a good memory for names," Laura assured him. He watched her as she spoke, looking for deception beneath her cheerful ease.

The Moon Will Look Strange

The blonde girl said, "You looking for somebody? She'll turn up sooner or later. That's what happens you know, you think you've said goodbye to somebody forever and you run into them three or four more times over the next couple months." She had the accentless voice Paul had come to associate with Americans from the west coast, and sure enough, she hailed from California.

"I've been travelling eighteen months," she told him as they shared a cigarette in the kitchen. "My friend was with me for a while, but she was raped in Spain. Hitchhiking. She went home after that. Before that we went all over Thailand, Malaysia, Nepal . . . you been to Southeast Asia?"

Paul said he hadn't.

"Man, that is a trip. Like, you wouldn't believe the drugs you can get there. And cheap! We stayed there a really long time, cause everything was cheap. Ireland costs too damn much."

Paul was taking a dislike to the girl, her coarse and abrasive manner, her bulky body. "When are you going home?" he asked, because somehow he felt the question might hurt her and he wanted to do just that.

She stopped, drew in a long drag of smoke and shrugged. "Dunno. Why would I want to do that?"

And so it went. "How long have you been staying here?" Paul asked Rosie once, and she just shook her head again and wouldn't talk to him anymore, just stared at the television as though mesmerized by the opening credits of a variety show. He dug through his address book but couldn't find the slip of paper where he'd written down the name of the place the night it had first been suggested. Perhaps it had been the Seashell, or the Albatross, in which case he was here *under false pretenses*. He said it to himself as a joke and didn't feel like laughing afterwards. If he wanted to stay in the area, it wasn't as though he had to remain *here*. He could ask around in town, perhaps get to the bottom of it, find the other, more pleasant hostel which he must have mistaken this one for. Surely no one would recommend this place to anybody.

For a long time no one arrived or left; and he eventually decided the five travelers he'd encountered the first night were long gone, for he never saw them again. The German girl and boy spoke only to one another, even avoiding eye contact so it was impossible to strike up a conversation naturally. Late one morning he caught sight of them climbing the cliffs again. He could catch up to them; perhaps they'd been here long enough to remember Alyssa. They could hardly avoid him when it was only the three of them in that deserted landscape. And he was lonely. The other visitors depressed him.

The cliffs were slick and dangerous, sprayed with sea water. The couple were far more sure-footed than he. He clambered across the rocks, ignoring caution, curiosity rendering him careless, and still kept them barely in sight. At last they seemed to slow a bit, so he was able to pick his way more carefully. A glorious view awaited him. Even in the gloom, or perhaps because of it, the seascape spread before him bespoke a beautiful desolation. It was in one of those moments, gazing about him, that he nearly lost them again.

The Moon Will Look Strange

They had turned down a track, though, a path down the cliff. The way looked even more treacherous than the one he'd taken here. Paul might be able to follow them down, but he couldn't imagine making his way back up again. For a long moment he stood watching them, helplessly. He realized that if they continued as they were going they might reach the stretch of shoreline, if indeed it were possible to reach it at all.

Surely that wasn't safe. The tides came in swiftly. They might be trapped, cut off; but his concern was not great enough to send him after them. Cowardice, he supposed. He winced as he thought the word, however accurate it might be. It was a trait he'd been able to conceal from Alyssa in the short time they'd known each other. It was just as well he'd lost her; she'd have found him out anyway.

Paul waited until the couple re-emerged on a narrow rocky spit of shoreline further to his left. Until now, he had not noticed the dinghy drawn up on the dry land there. The two of them shoved it off into the water, and the boy clambered in first, then helped the girl in. They both began to row, out toward sea. Away toward the light that beamed feebly but steadily somewhere in the mist.

*

Eventually he lost track altogether of how many days he'd been at the hostel, and he approached Mrs. Ryan with some bills again. She took some of them, and pushed back some change, which he pocketed. A thick haze had settled over everything, and Paul sensed October closing in on November: dank winter overcome the Emerald Isle. Now he woke shivering in the night. The comforter provided by the Seagull was insufficient against the chill of the unheated room. David began to have nightmares. Sometimes he would cry out in his sleep and thrash about. He still went out some evenings, always asking Paul to go along, but Paul had the feeling David wasn't going to the pub at all. He saw him in town on a trip he made in himself, to purchase some supplies. David walked across the square with his overcoat flapping down around his ankles, and Paul called out to him, but David either didn't hear or ignored him.

It was only the four of them left there: he and David, and Rosie, and the American girl. He'd not noticed when the girls from Cork went away but he had not seen them in a very long time. It no longer seemed curious to him that they rarely interacted, moving through the days as though each had erected an invisible but impenetrable barrier against the others.

One day Paul found himself sitting on his bunk composing a letter to his sister. He broke down crying. He wanted to go home. He paced up and down the room, cursing this grey inhospitable place, these people who flitted like ghosts here. He felt frantic to phone the airlines, to go screaming cross the Atlantic and home again. He became panicked. Some nights before he'd dreamed of a mushroom cloud, and he wept, imagining this the last place left in all the world, and them the only people. He finished his letter to Robin, assuring her he'd be home soon, he just needed to make arrangements. "As a matter of fact," he concluded optimistically, "you'll probably already have heard from me by phone by the time you get this!"

The words would be a talisman. He gave the letter to Mrs. Ryan for posting. Afterwards he thought better of it, but when he asked her about it she stared at him with stolid incomprehension and said, "Postman took it." She still wore that scarf twisted defiantly about her neck, and Paul realized he no longer needed to look at any sort of label on it to confirm that it belonged to Alyssa. And he'd lost so much time here there was no hope of ever catching up to her.

"I'm heading back soon," he told David, who did his exercises faithfully this morning as every morning. David lifted his head to look at him, red-faced.

"You'll be leaving, then?"

"Looks that way," Paul said. "Gotta get back to school. See my family again. My sister was pregnant last I heard. Probably I'm an uncle now." It felt funny to say it.

He walked into town and checked the bus schedules, arranged to take one into Tralee and from there to Limerick. The lazy appeal of hitchhiking had vanished. He thanked Mrs. Ryan for her hospitality and informed her he'd be leaving early the next morning.

*

The wind and the sea woke him in the night, just as they had the first night he spent here.

This night, however, was moonless; no figures on the water to frighten him, no restless breathing in the room about him. But the sea was louder than ever before, the crashing of its waves palpably close, as though he could reach out through the window and dip his hand in those cold waters.

*

Paul woke again at dawn, before the others, and slipped outside.

He'd smoked his last cigarette the night before, and so he stood staring out at the water, nothing to do but gaze at the beam of light.

He climbed up the cliffs, as the German girl and her boyfriend had done, and scrambled down the slick path to the shore.

He found the dinghy waiting there for him. A solid, wooden vessel, splintery planks for seats. At one time he wouldn't have trusted it to take him across a pond.

But this was different.

Paul zipped his coat tighter against the winds which blew in across the water, and pulled on gloves. Rowing was difficult when the cold numbed your hands, though he wasn't really sure how much rowing he would have to do.

He pushed the boat most of the way into the water. He tried to climb in, still standing on dry land, but the boat tipped sideways and threatened to spill him into the sea as soon as he transferred all his weight. He would have to wade in, up to his shins. He gasped as the icy waters lapped at his jeans and seeped through to his skin.

Paul couldn't remember having handled a boat at all before. After a couple of false starts, in which he merely bobbed on the water and went in circles, he got the hang of it. Strong, slow, steady strokes sent him gliding against the current, against the constant breaking of the waves in towards land.

In the distance, he could see it, the beam of light, guiding his way. A chilling gust blew across him. Inside the jacket he was sweating, but his face, his lips and nose and ears, had gone numb in the cold.

Travelling, he'd always tried to remain on the move.

Paul kept rowing. The wind stung his eyes and extracted tears. Soon, his destination would become clear. The mist closed behind him and the land slipped away, and the glow beckoned him onward in the grey winter morn.

Lynda E. Rucker

The Chance Walker

This whole country is haunted. Can't you feel it?

The chance walker slouches as he moves up the sidewalk below her kitchen window, engulfed in a crumpled brown suit and a shabby hat, smoke swirling from a cigarette she cannot see because his head is lowered, and then he's gone, vanished into the shadows further up the street. He never wears a coat. He never seems to need one.

To fear. *Bat se.* I fear. *Boji.*

Kathleen, poring over her lesson plans, has made a long list of food and restaurant related nouns and written them on small scraps of paper in preparation for a game the following day. She is uncertain as to how it will be received. The informality of the language school where she teaches is an affront to some of the students there, Czechs who bristle at attempts to mimic American informality with the casual use of their first names, with games and songs alongside serious study. "This is for children," one man had told her, disgusted, and she has to agree it's not the most efficient use of their time. But she has been hired as the token American, which is to say she must be spirited and fun-loving and spontaneous, even when she feels anything but. So a game it will be.

The Moon Will Look Strange

And someone's hammering at the door of her flat. Kathleen hesitates; it's got to be another resident, because it's late and the building has a locked entrance. She can't muster the energy to cope with the language barrier, and instead presses her face against the window. The chance walker is back, and her hot breath clouds the pane so that now it's a ghostly night he tramps through. The knocking ceases and his footsteps are audible again until the sound of a car engine overtakes them.

Bal, bani. You fear, she fears.

Headlights swing round the corner and pin him momentarily against the building on the other side of the street. As the car dwindles away into the distance, the chance walker is gone.

But the rapping at the door has commenced once again. Kathleen heaves herself up from the table, relenting. She fumbles with the lock and when the door swings open there's a girl on the other side of it, tall, in her mid-teens, smiling broadly to reveal small, even teeth. The girl is draped in an enormous long coat and has brown hair pinned up at the nape of her neck. Kathleen has a curious sensation in the split second it takes for her eyes to settle on the visitor that she somehow *changes*, that something smaller and hairier and not quite a girl is waiting there. And there is a sense of crowding on the landing, as though the girl is pressed in on all sides by a multiplicity of visitors.

"Hello," says the girl who is most certainly a girl, and clearly all alone. Her English is precise and perfectly enunciated. "My name is Renata. You are a teacher, aren't you? I would like to learn English with you."

"Now?" Kathleen says stupidly, sleepily, then collects herself. She has encountered it before—the flawless speaker convinced of his or her inadequacy. It seems unfair to charge them anything, and yet they always insist.

"It's a little bit late," she tells the girl. "Why don't we make an appointment for you to come back another time and we can discuss it?" Czechs are in love with appointments, she's found.

Disappointment flickers across Renata's face. Kathleen notices that she has a large book tucked beneath one arm and nearly relents, but she doesn't want students thinking they can drop in anytime for an impromptu session.

"Tomorrow," she adds, by way of softening the dismissal.

Renata waits, frowns a little. "The same time tomorrow?"

"A little earlier, please. Eight o'clock?"

Renata thrusts the book at Kathleen. "I want to be a doctor. I will study in London. Or maybe America."

It's an antique edition of *Gray's Anatomy*. "Where did you get this?" Kathleen eyes the copyright date—1918—and is dubious about its usefulness, although it's not like the makeup of the human body has *changed* in the last century.

The Moon Will Look Strange

"My grandfather. He is a doctor as well." Renata goes on to explain: she hopes Kathleen will assist her in the pronunciation of words like pericardium, epithelium, and medulla oblongata. She's undaunted by Kathleen's ignorance of the subject. Kathleen decides to postpone a discussion about the relative merits of an anatomy book nearly one hundred years out of date.

"Let's try it for a little while and see how it works out," she tells Renata. She wants to leave an opening for the girl to bow out of the lessons without embarrassment, something she will surely want to do once she realizes Kathleen's useless at biology.

"Good," says Renata, nodding, and "Fine. Yes, thank you," and Kathleen, nodding as well but yawning, too, shuts the door and resists the urge to open it immediately and make sure the landing is empty again. It occurs to her then to wonder who told Renata an English teacher lived there, or how she got into the building in the first place.

*

The chance walker. Kathleen has seen his picture in a book of paintings she almost bought in Prague, but she set it down while she was browsing in another part of the shop and couldn't find it again. He was walking through an urban misty landscape that was fading at the edges just like Boleslav does on the coldest days.

It's because of the chance walker that she first found her flat.

She has been there for fourteen days. Once it had been a grand residence—before the Velvet Revolution, and the Prague Spring, and the Communists, and the wars. Since then it's been carved up into pieces like a jigsaw puzzle. It's located in what remains of the old town, now just a single street and a crumbling city wall beyond. Winter has lasted forever, frozen walkways and frigid air. The apartment is overheated.

She has yet to figure out the bricked-up window in the bedroom. A crack jags diagonally across the glass, as though the brick wall has grown there, and is exerting a mounting pressure. The window faces a narrow alley between her building and the one next door, which is fronted by a disintegrating stone façade. The alleyway is inaccessible, blocked by a high wooden padlocked fence, so Kathleen doesn't know if it's a wall built from the ground up or if it's only her window that's bricked over. She had hoped to speak to the distracted older lady who'd shown her the flat in the first place, but that woman—a small brunette with an accent, not Czech, that Kathleen couldn't place—seems to have vanished. Kathleen had tried the number the woman had given her. Either she'd mangled her pronunciation of the questions she'd carefully prepared ahead of time, or the person at the other end of the line was just irascible. The exchange had ended in mutual incomprehension and a phone banged down at the other end. She tried again some days later. This time the phone simply rang and rang, and then the ringing ended and a hollow rushing sound filled the receiver.

The Moon Will Look Strange

She ought to have known better. Her keys had arrived at the school by mail, swaddled in layers of crumpled tissue paper and stuffed inside a dirty manila envelope. A smudged form that looked as though it had been printed on a mimeograph machine informed her of the address to which she was to send her rent. She has not been able to find the physical location that corresponds with the address, but that is no real surprise and she has not tried very hard. It's a safe bet that doing so would leave her lost in a sea of concrete *panelaks*, the cheap high-rise Communist-era housing that swallowed up neighborhoods and villages throughout the country in decades past.

So it is that after fourteen days Kathleen has not asked anyone about the bricked-up window, and then there is the door in the foyer. The door is painted shut, or hammered closed, or is someone's peculiar idea of a cosmetic fixture. The door has a plain wooden knob and will not budge when she tugs on it. She might as well be pulling at a piece of the wall.

She would like someone to tell her what's on the other side.

There are other problems. An irregular patch of wall in the living room, a recessed square that she imagines is the boarded-over opening to a dumbwaiter. At night she can hear it, sliding up and down, sending goods to other parts of the house, perhaps, or people riding from the floors below to linger in the shaft just beyond the walls of her living room. She stands motionless in the middle of her flat at such times, waiting for some sign as to what she should do next. The dumbwaiter always outlasts her, though, and she grows weary before it moves again.

Once in bed, she hears it shuddering back into motion.

Kathleen cannot remember noticing any of these peculiarities when she'd first looked the place over. She'd been in a fog, true, distressed about a vicious fight with Ben, her ears still ringing with the words they'd used to sting at one another. She had raced out of the flat they shared—she'd lived in a *panelak* herself then—and had run until she couldn't draw in breath anymore. At the edge of the old town she'd bent over at the waist, gasping at cold shocks of air, fighting sobs, when she saw him for the first time, making his way up the broken stone street. She named him right away, *chance walker*, just like the painting, and he possessed the same quiet dignity as the man in the book, with his plain suit and deliberate gait. His presence made her feel ashamed of her own histrionics, and as her breath slowed, her tears dried, she wondered, *What must he have lost over these years?* A person ought to be left defeated, beaten, across decades of war and revolution and suppression and sorrow, yet nothing in his demeanor suggested such a thing.

She followed him partway up the street until the woman called to her in English. "Yes? You are looking for a flat?" the woman shouted. "Yes. Yes, I am," Kathleen called back, and the woman laughed when she added, "Yes, I want it. I'll take it."

"Don't you want to have a look around it first?"

Kathleen didn't; didn't care, really, what it looked like, as long as it could be hers, and quickly, but she stepped inside for a perfunctory glance.

The Moon Will Look Strange

It struck her, then. "I didn't have an appointment to see a flat, actually," she said to the woman, "Were you waiting on someone else?" But the woman assured her no, that Kathleen was just the person she was expecting. It didn't seem right at first, to have snatched it from under the nose of someone who'd legitimately been interested in the place, who probably had made arrangements and then been delayed. Later on she would decide the woman was right after all. The flat ought to have been hers from the start.

*

The next morning begins with one of Kathleen's favorite classes, four housewives learning English for fun. They bring in glossy gossip magazines and the five of them *tsk* over the antics of the royal families of Europe. They fill Kathleen in on the doings of the Czech Republic's top voice dubbers for foreign television shows, stars in their own right.

But it's downhill after that. She leads another class through a boring reading exercise, and they gaze at her with blank expressions until one says, "Colleen never did it that way." Colleen is the teacher they had the previous year. She lives in Vienna now and tutors the children of diplomats and wealthy businessmen. Kathleen is often compared to her unfavorably by this particular group. She has never met her but hates her with a kind of casual offhandedness.

And then she's asked to substitute for one of the afternoon prep classes. She used to teach one of these herself until she requested a change; Ben had some of the same students at the local high school, and she feared they might bring news of him through a kind of osmosis. Traces of him might cling to their sweaters and coats and hair like the snow did, and she couldn't bear it.

"Okay, then, Kathy?" Ludmila's the stylish, energetic woman who runs the school, dedicated, kind, shortening to the hated diminutive because somewhere along the way she's gotten the idea that all Americans love nicknames. It's not okay. It's a class Kathleen has never liked. She only wonders why they don't remind her more of herself at that age. She imagines there's something altogether more knowing behind their eyes, a cool sophistication that she still lacks. They are teenagers who never knew the world their parents must weary them with stories about, teenagers for whom tales of interrogations and banned literature and secret police must seem as distant as segregated schools had to her, growing up.

Ben told her she was being paranoid once she admitted she felt like they were laughing when she turned her back on them. He'd taken to life in Boleslav, though, and she had not. She saw only grey, unfriendly people, while he made friends right away.

Ludmila is concerned about where she is living. That part of town is unsafe, she says. Where precisely is this flat again? She shakes her head when Kathleen tells her. She didn't know there were any flats to let in the old town. And she isn't finished with her. "Klara tells me you stopped going to language lessons, Kathy. Are you quitting the class?"

The language feels like a cruel trick, with its declensions and cases, genitive and accusative and dative and then everybody uses so much slang that none of it ends up making sense anyway. The grammar's so convoluted that even simple sentences confound her, and the townspeople are unused to hearing their language butchered by foreigners and tend to be unforgiving of mistakes.

"No," Kathleen says, weary. "I'm just taking some time off. I have a new student. Maybe you know her. Renata, I don't know her last name. Tall, about sixteen, wants to be a doctor?" But Ludmila shakes her head.

"It's weird," Kathleen says, "she just came to my door. She heard an English teacher lived there."

"Boleslav is not Prague," Ludmila says with a smile. "It is still unusual to have Americans with us here. Germans, Russians, Yugoslavians, we are accustomed to that."

"I'm still studying some on my own," Kathleen says. It's a little bit insane if she thinks about it too hard, how thoroughly her ignorance of the language isolates her from even casual interactions with strangers. She may pass two men with raised voices and can't tell if they are angry at one another or merely opinionated; she cannot ask for directions or order food in a restaurant without the help of a phrasebook and can only inquire about the time if she spends several minutes putting the question together beforehand. Once she had Ben, at least, to talk to in the evenings. Now that she lives alone she thinks if it weren't for her job at the school she might disappear altogether.

*

Lynda E. Rucker

Kathleen walks home in an icy dusk.

The woman across the landing always wears curlers in her hair. She scuttles; there is no other word for it. She is slight and washed-out looking, and if ever she is on the landing when Kathleen leaves, or comes home, she scuttles back in. Tonight as Kathleen mounts the stairs she only sees the woman's back, and the door slams shut before she reaches the top. She is, at least, an improvement over Kathleen's last neighbor. That woman had hated them, Kathleen was sure of it. She had lied to the landlord, complained that Kathleen and Ben weren't taking their turns cleaning the landing and stairs as all residents were required to do. She would call down to her friends in the morning when she saw them walking past. "*Ahoj!*" she would shout, eight floors down into the courtyard, and the sound echoed. Kathleen had tried to avoid looking out the window there at all, the sight depressed her so: dead leaves and ice, the flicker of TV screens in windows, "Skins" and "Anti-Nazi League" and "Nirvana" graffitied on the wall below.

"I bet she was an informant before, don't you think? Spying on all her neighbors?" Kathleen said to Ben, and he said she wasn't being fair, that you couldn't make a judgement about a person like that. He made her feel petty and vengeful.

Kathleen has never seen any other residents of her current building, or even heard them, walking or talking on the stairs or the sidewalk outside.

Renata arrives at the agreed-upon time. She will not shed her coat, in spite of the blasting radiator.

The Moon Will Look Strange

She sits across from Kathleen at the kitchen table, her face wan and small above the voluminous folds of cloth. She opens the book at random and begins to read a passage. "The axillary artery, the continuation of the subclavian, commences at the outer border of the first rib." "Wait," Kathleen says, but Renata, perhaps not understanding, carries on undaunted. Kathleen suppresses a yawn, lulled by the repetition of unfamiliar words. Renata might be speaking some other language. Rain patters dully against the window, indicating the temperature's finally slipped above freezing. Later the walkways will be sheets of ice.

"*Wait*," Kathleen says again, and this time Renata does pause. *Tap, tap, tap* go the footsteps outside, and the chance walker rounds the corner. The rain doesn't seem to touch him at all, and Kathleen wishes for streetlights so she can be certain.

"He is only my grandfather, waiting for my lesson to finish," Renata says. "He told me I should go to you to improve my English."

"But I don't know him at all."

Renata shrugs. "It does not matter. You don't have to know something for it to know you."

"Someone," Kathleen corrects her, "know *someone*," and later on, after Renata has gone and she's lying in bed with her back to the bricked-up window she wonders if Renata did mean some*thing* after all.

*

Kathleen wakes the following overcast

Saturday and finds she can't stop thinking of Ben. Maybe the time apart has been good. She had been hard, no, impossible, no, nearly impossible to live with. And she misses him. She misses shopping with him at the grocery store, where they'd surreptitiously consult their dictionaries to decipher words on the packaging, making sure not to purchase lard instead of butter as they'd done their first week there. She misses sharing an unreasonable outrage at the way the stern old pensioners would sidle in front of you to break in line. Those things had seemed funny when they did them together; now they just depress her. She misses their trips to Prague, strolling along the Charles Bridge and exploring the winding streets of the old city, the bookshop where she'd bought the Mucha prints and the old man had wrapped them for her like a present with careful trembling hands, and the view from the castle, a sea of crooked red rooftops.

  She sets off in the direction of the school and turns toward the outdoor market, where Czechs and Romanys and Vietnamese immigrants are hawking cheaply made clothing and bootleg cassettes and CDs; past the 24-hour bar where factory workers fresh off a shift are downing enormous bottles of Pilsner at nine in the morning, past the bus station and then she cannot remember which way to turn next. Here is the non-stop, where you could buy something to eat late at night if you could remember the word for it—all the food is kept behind a counter and guarded by an unsmiling matron—and now a salon, the cinemas ahead. She sees the high-rise housing beyond, stretching all the way out to the hills where

The Moon Will Look Strange

World War Two era bunkers dot the landscape, constructed in anticipation of a German invasion and never even used. Now she's lost among the *panelaks* and she's not even certain she's anywhere near her old building, and it's so cold the inside of her nose feels frozen. A woman beating a rug in the stretch of dead grass between buildings is staring at her. Kathleen only wants to go home.

The weather is worsening, too. Heavy black clouds are rolling in, and freezing rain has begun to blow against her face. Kathleen makes her way down a hill to the Knedliky, the supermarket where they'd shopped together, but she stands helpless in front of it, turning a few times and unable to recall which direction would take her back to the place they'd shared.

She leaves the Knedliky and heads to the center of town, pelted by rain. She spies a restaurant and stumbles inside for shelter. But it's not a restaurant, it's a bar, filled with men, mostly drinking alone and in silence, a reek of despair about the place. They swivel round and stare at her, hostile. She steps in a puddle of vomit as she backs out the door. She's freezing and exhausted and soaking wet when she finds herself trudging down the broken stone street of the old town again at last, and she sees him ahead then, the chance walker, small and bent over against the wind.

He's gone long before she reaches the entrance of her building. Renata is there, however, wearing the same overcoat as always, patiently gazing up at Kathleen's window, her back to the street. When Kathleen says her name she jumps.

"I didn't know we were meeting today," Kathleen says.

"Of course," Renata tells her, and Kathleen isn't sure if she means *Of course you didn't know* or *Of course we were meeting*. Kathleen remembers again that it's important to be firm.

But, "Come on in" is what she says, and Renata trots up the stairs behind her, and it's horrible, having her here at a time like this, when she's cold and exhausted and afraid, and the last thing she wants to do is talk about anatomy. Then they are inside the flat and she's making them coffee and she's talking too much without meaning to at all, she's telling Renata how she conjugates the words for being afraid like a kind of mantra, to keep it at bay, *bat se*, *boji*. She tells her how the low-grade fear has been a part of her for so long that she can't recall its origins, or how she felt before it lodged itself inside her. Was it after she came to Boleslav, or had the fear been with her even back home?

She can't stop talking now. The fear seems to consume everything she does, she explains. "Look," she tells Renata, and tosses a letter from her mother in front of the girl. Renata does not touch the letter, in which she would have read Kathleen's mother saying that she sounds so unhappy, why doesn't she come home? She makes home sound like a place Kathleen would want to go back to, which isn't the case. Because Renata won't look at the letter, Kathleen picks it up and reads parts of it to her. Partway through the letter her mother switches from cajoling to admonishments, even accusations: you're trying to run away from us. You can't escape forever. The counselor says this is no solution. Implied: *We made you how you are, damaged you just so, and only we can understand you.*

Renata nods with sympathy and pours the coffee, spoons in the sugar cubes.

Kathleen pulls herself together abruptly with the first bitter swallow. She feels vaguely feverish and wonders if she isn't coming down with something. In the midst of it all Renata has finally shrugged off her coat, and Kathleen sees why she hesitated for so long to do so: beneath it she's wearing a plain old-fashioned dress in contrast to the cheap but trendy clothes the teenagers at school own. Something occurs to Kathleen.

"Do you go to school around here?"

Renata shakes her head. "Not any longer," she says, so sadly that Kathleen would think she was exaggerating her dismay but for the dejection on her face. "Anyway, my grandfather says a woman cannot be a doctor."

Kathleen makes a mental note to ask Ludmila about the girl. There is the difficulty of being in a foreign country: what is the Czech equivalent of Child Protective Services? Does such a thing even exist? And does what seems to her a clear case of neglect count as one over here? Kathleen reminds herself that she has no inkling of the family's circumstances, that perhaps it's only Renata and her grandfather eking out an existence in a strain of poverty which didn't exist in this country before the Communists fell.

As if reading her mind, Renata offers, "We used to live here once, my family and I."

"Here? In this building?" Kathleen asks, and the girl nods.

"All of us," she says, "my whole family, we were all together then. Do you know the history of this part of the city? Near the end of the war the old town was bombed. We never found out if the Germans or the Allies did it." She waved a hand toward the north. "Just beyond, in that direction, is the old Jewish, what is it in English? Section? The part where they lived. Today there are no Jews left in Boleslav."

"I would like to speak to your grandfather sometime," Kathleen says, reasserting herself as the teacher, hoping Renata only understood about half of what she'd been telling her. She'd been a little hysterical. She would have to watch herself.

"Let's read my book," Renata suggests in response. Her voice is dry as she stumbles over the unfamiliar terminology. "The tibial nerve descends through the middle of the fossa, lying under the deep fascia and crossing the vessels posteriorly from the lateral to the medial side." Renata's quiet halting tone is somehow soothing, and Kathleen forgets to correct her. The tap tap tap of the chance walker rouses her.

"Maybe I could speak to him now," Kathleen says, but Renata looks so alarmed at the thought that she drops it.

After the girl leaves she realizes she has an empty afternoon and evening stretching away ahead of her. She spends a little time at an Internet café near the school, writing to her mother, carefully, cheerfully, reading and re-reading before she hits "send" to make sure nothing can slip between the lines this time. It is easier to be glib in the not-quite-

The Moon Will Look Strange

real world of electronic communication. Something about pen and ink seems to bind her more closely to the truth, which never does anyone much good.

Here is one truth: there was the grief counselor she'd been dragged to with the rest of them (she only went for the sake of her younger brother and sister) who insisted they all just ought to "open up." As though abandonment and death can be fixed by talking about it enough. She is reminded of illustrations in the anatomy book: the way the insides look, the yards and yards of intestines and the blood moving endlessly through the body and the pockets of soft useless fat. She is reminded of how their father might have looked after he shot himself, although none of them will know, because they hadn't been the ones who found him—that had been their stepmother, a woman whom they all dislike, and they are confused because they can't help feeling sorry for her now. *I'll stay closed thank you very much.*

Her little brother was setting fires and breaking windows—and once, nearly, their sister's arm, but that could be said to have been an accident.

They were all of them broken in all kinds of places.

*

Ludmila asks to meet with her, and they do so in a small room off the reception area of the school. Her face exhibits nothing but concern. They are worried about her, she assures Kathleen. It seems Ben has something to do with this as well. He has tried to stop in to see her and she will not answer the door when it rings. It is difficult, Ludmila says, to be so far from home. Kathleen wants to correct her, explain that it is actually very easy. Ludmila speaks in a soothing way, but Kathleen looks for the words behind the words, just as she does in her mother's letters. The school will be closing for one week's break. Ludmila is suggesting that perhaps Kathleen should take a break of her own. A trip to Germany or Austria or even London might do her good. Afterwards they can discuss what role Kathleen might play at the school. Perhaps a lighter schedule, Ludmila suggests. Perhaps an assistant with the younger children. It will be easier for them to arrange for someone to take over Kathleen's current classes than to never know whether Kathleen will show up to teach, she says gently, without reprove—but Kathleen hears it anyway.

Hears it, and is surprised. She had not realized that she had missed so much time from her classes. She walks home wondering if she's been fired, wondering what she'll do with herself in the empty days ahead.

And this young girl she has been tutoring—who is she, and her grandfather? Ludmila does not know them, and she knows everyone in town. The other teachers at the school have not heard of them either. They are not Romany, are they—Ludmila says it neutrally, but Kathleen's sure there's something ugly behind it. No, she assures her, they aren't Romany, they are solid Czechs. The grandfather was a doctor.

Ludmila shakes her head.

Call Ben. That's the last thing Ludmila says to her. You should call Ben, he misses you, I think.

The Moon Will Look Strange

*

She can hear the chance walker on the way home, even though he's nowhere to be seen. His footsteps rattle in the street and creep up behind her. Something snatches at her ankle and she nearly cries out, but it's just a sheet of old newspaper blown from the gutter. Tap, tap, tap. *Bat se, boji, bal, bani.*

Renata is waiting outside the building again. Kathleen wants to tell her to go away, but instead she invites her in. Once upstairs she understands that this is a mistake. She will never persuade Renata to go home now.

Kathleen says, "I've been talking to Ludmila, at the school. She says she doesn't know your family at all."

Renata responds with a sad little smile. "We have been away for a long time," she says.

Kathleen remembers her first sight of Renata, the sense that she was not a girl at all, and the others who were with her. The *Gray's Anatomy* like incantations. The heat in the flat like a fever.

Someone's outside the building, ringing the bell. It occurs to Kathleen that until now, no one has come to visit her besides Renata. Whatever Ben had told Ludmila, she's sure she's not heard the bell in all the time she's been there. And now someone's shouting up at the window. Calling her name. He's using a voice that sounds like Ben's. She won't let him in.

Lynda E. Rucker

"Kathleen?" says the thing with the Ben-voice. "I know you're in there! I saw you walking up the street!"

It is Ben. And it's like a dream, the kind where Kathleen can't move no matter how much she wants to.

"Kathleen! Let me in!"

Kathleen says to Renata, "Are you ever afraid?" Renata doesn't say anything back. Instead she opens her book and begins to read.

Just before Christmas, one of the teachers Ben worked with had taken them for a drive in the north. They'd set out before dawn, and stopped in a village near a ski resort, where they'd bought warm loaves of bread for breakfast and the other teacher, Pavel, had insisted that they each down a shot of vodka to fortify themselves against the cold. They'd stopped again someplace deep in the mountains and trudged across a snowy field. Pavel pointed toward the hills. "That's Poland, right there." Kathleen had left the two of them, her boots crunching in the snow as she went forward, and gazed into the darkened forest. That's when she heard Pavel say it.

"This whole country is haunted. Can't you feel it?"

Ben had said once that the past was alive here in a way it could never be in America, America where you went to shed your skin and forget who you were and where you came from. Here, people were crushed by the past. Kathleen remembered old photos she'd seen of Czech resistance fighters, people younger than herself, imagined that their choices and fates conferred a kind of nobility to their doomed features

The Moon Will Look Strange

that she and her peers would forever lack.

She could picture the ill-fated Polish army amassing there in front of her on horseback, preparing their futile defense against invading tanks. Nothing was left of any of it now but the soft sighs of wind down the corridors of abandoned bunkers.

Later, on the drive back to Boleslav, it began to snow again. Those first flakes heralded a terrible storm and all across Europe people died, stranded in their automobiles. Kathleen watched the snow swirling through darkened woods that crowded them on either side of the roads, watched it make shapes in the dark.

Renata reads feverishly, bent over her book and hardly mouthing each word before stumbling on to the next one. Ben is still outside the building, now pacing under the window and stamping in the cold, now stepping back to cup his hands round his mouth and shout her name, now pounding at the door again.

Once, Kathleen rises and thinks to slip only as far as the foyer, perhaps to open the door only a very little and see what's there. "You must sit," Renata insists, "my grandfather will be here soon." It is very cold in the flat. It is so cold that Kathleen's breath is showing in little warm puffs of air. Renata says, "It isn't long now." There is ice on the surface of the coffee in their cups. The dumbwaiter is rising slowly in its shaft.

The bricks are tumbling from the bedroom window; she can hear the glass shattering and wonders what's on the other side. Renata's mouth is still moving but without sound, faster and faster, and she tears a page in her rush to turn it. Kathleen's teeth are chattering together. Sweat beads on Renata's brow, Ben is shouting but his voice is far away, the chance walker is tapping his way up the stairs, someone is scuttling down from above. And now there are visitors on the landing, a whole horde of them, and Renata stops reading at last and says, "It's time. You can let them in now," and so she does.

The Moon Will Look Strange

They were draining the fish pond in the tiny walled garden outside his window. Colin awoke to the sound of their voices, Jimena, who owned the house with her husband Tomas, and that of Madih, the young Moroccan man who carried out repairs around the property. Colin flung open the wooden shutters and his first thought was that Samantha would be outraged—even at the savage age of six and a half she couldn't bear to see any living thing suffer—and then he remembered, and wondered where such a cruel and unbidden thought had come from. Not for one moment, night or day, sleeping or awake, did he ever forget that she was dead. Not even in his dreams.

He shouted at them, "Why are you killing the fish? Does Tomas know what you're doing?"

Jimena and Madih looked back at him, startled and uncomprehending. Colin backed away from the window and realized he was naked. He fumbled for a pair of shorts, fought with the heavy wooden door of his room and staggered out into the burning Granada sunshine.

"The fish!" he shouted again. He imagined them, the brilliant orange goldfish gasping and dying on the concrete floor of the pool. They gaped at him, then Jimena said something sharp to Madih and they turned around. "Que?" he said, mustering one of the only Spanish words that he knew. They ignored him, and it wasn't as if he'd be able to understand them if they responded anyway. His will flagged along with his indignation, faded so completely that he lacked even the gumption to take his lunatic and half-dressed self back indoors. He stood there instead, under the burning sun, watching them kill the fish, and thought of Samantha.

*

He'd never meant to end up in Spain. That was an understatement, the punctuation to a whole long series of understatements, of things not meant to happen. After Ann left him he'd gone to the airport in a kind of fugue, thinking only to get away. He carried nothing with him save for his passport and wallet, and he paid cash for a one-way ticket to London. Just like that, and he felt like giggling with glee at how easy it all was. He supposed the purchase would see him flagged in a Homeland Security file somewhere, just the sort of thing he'd have railed against once, when he had time to feel outrage about anything besides what had been taken from him. As the green Oregon landscape fell away below him a sense of lightness seized him: he thought of his things, all the stuff you accumulate living a life, abandoned in the little apartment off Belmont Avenue that he and Ann and Samantha had shared, and of the bar at Luna filling up and him just <u>not there</u>, not pulling pints of Black Butte, not mixing shit like lemon drops for customers as high-maintenance as their drink orders. He thought of other places where he would not be, like he was shuffling a series of snapshots: he would not be at the Mount Tabor Pub, or flipping through stacks of vinyl at Music Millennium, or at the dinosaur display at the science museum with Samantha. He imagined rubbing each image out as he thought it. He was a man with no past now.

At Heathrow the noise and lights had hurt his ears. He slept for a while in an arrivals lounge and then spoke to an Easy Jet agent who said she could get him on a cheap flight to Granada right away if he got himself over to Stansted immediately. His flight was only about two-thirds full, so he was able to ensconce himself in the back far from the mirth and drunkenness of the holidaymakers claiming the rest of the seats. He knew next to nothing about Spain, except that if he could manage to make it to the tip he could catch a ferry to Morocco, where he could disappear. Like Burroughs or Bowles, lost in Marrakesh, or even deeper into Africa, where tourists never trod. It wasn't so easy as it once was to vanish off the face of the earth, but he felt certain he could do it there.

But first things first: he needed sleep. He took a bus into the city and got off at the top of a narrow walled cobblestone street. The flight of stairs to his left led straight into the past: a maze of walled, whitewashed streets, ancient and defiant, where the last of the Moors fled as their world vanished around them, in the shadow of the magnificent Alhambra Palace just across the canyon, an implacable yet ghostly reminder of what was, what might have been and what would never be. A fitting place for him to disappear in as well, in the soothing, dizzying, exotic maze the bus driver had called the Albaicín. A scrawny graffitied cat, scrawled in various stages of distress at this turn and that, wore a legend reminding him that "Fumar Mata" and that much he could figure out because he'd seen it on a crumpled cigarette pack—smoking kills. Or not, he reasoned. Samantha hadn't been a smoker, after all. At six, she'd not had time to pick up the habit. He rounded a corner and saw the poor feline hanging from a chalk noose. The white walls crumbled round boarded up windows, and he dodged dog shit smeared on cobblestones. He couldn't understand the words scrawled on walls but images of the Pope as devil, and of Che Guevara, did the speaking for him. He followed a trail of Arabic script. Was he already in Morocco? He reeled, feverish, as the sun climbed. He did not know what he ought to do. A child's laughter mocked him round corners but when he tried to follow no one was there.

At last he came upon a massive wooden door with a sign above: he couldn't read what it said but someone had plastered a Lonely Planet sticker on an upstairs window. He hammered at the door for a long time, until a stooped Spanish man he later came to know as Tomas appeared. Colin managed to stammer out a request for a room, which Tomas fortunately understood. Colin pressed his remaining euros into Tomas's hand and followed him through the doorway, and then another, and into the walled garden. In the room off the goldfish pond he eased his sweaty body between thick white sheets. When he woke it was dark and he was starving. He didn't know where he was, and he thought, I've done something insane. For one instant panic rose like bile

The Moon Will Look Strange

in the back of his throat and then, his heart still hammering, he laughed. Why not do something insane, when fate had dealt him such an insane turn in the first place? Colin glanced at his wristwatch and saw he'd slept, not for the day, but the day and the night and the next day, and now it was night again. He stumbled out of his room and the moon hung high above him and he heard Yarrow's voice: You will know, he said, you will know because the moon will look strange.

*

    Colin finally went inside and brewed strong black coffee, two cups in the dark before opening the windows again and peering out at the fish pond carnage. They had a large trash can, filled with water, and were scooping the fish out in nets. Not killing them after all, then. They were merely cleaning the pond, which was green with algae and might have been bottomless for all you could see beneath the surface. He briefly considered feeling foolish but concluded it was a waste of his time. Jimena and Madih thought he was a lunatic anyway. And who was he to say they were wrong?

    He donned a shirt which didn't smell too badly and headed out without another word to them. Once again he'd slept much of the day away, and the sun was low in the sky when he slipped into a bar off the Plaza Larga, where he stood at the counter, smoking cigarettes and drinking beer and gobbling up free plates of tapas. The alcohol didn't do much, just numbed his senses enough to make it bearable.

Clearly the harder stuff was easy enough to come by: he needed only to look at the wasted, furtive desperate faces of some passersby, of squatters from the abandoned Romany caves up in the hills, to be certain. But he was afraid of getting trapped here. He ought to get a move on in fact, tomorrow or next day at the latest—so he kept telling himself. He imagined someone would come for him—and by someone he meant Ann and her family—tipped off by a trail of debit card deductions from a rapidly shrinking account.

But no one did. Still, this wasn't even close to the oblivion he'd dreamed. He had once seen a program on television about nomads in the Moroccan desert. He wouldn't need euros or his debit card and no one would think to look for him there. His thoughts spiraled down like this, as they always did when he drank at the bar off the Plaza Larga. Other bars inspired other types of thoughts, and all were good enough for what he really needed, which was not to think about why he couldn't seem to get up in the morning and stick out his thumb and hitch a ride farther south. Because he thought Samantha might be lost somewhere in the Albaicín, and that was crazy, and yet he wasn't leaving if there was any possibility that he could be right. Yarrow had never said how he would know, except for the part about the moon. But Colin knew it was her. It wasn't only seeing: he'd glimpsed her in his peripheral vision, sure, rounding corners—the heel of her yellow sandals, a flash of the blue T-shirt she'd got down at Newport the last time the three of them went whale watching, the one she loved so much they'd buried her in it. He could smell

The Moon Will Look Strange

her, too. Sometimes he could hear her, the soft songs she'd whisper under her breath when she played by herself or was otherwise occupied and unaware of anyone's attention on her. Any time after dusk was a good time for her, and so he liked to be good and drunk by the time dusk rolled around. Because while thinking of her made him realize what people really meant when they said dumb meaningless things like "He loved her more than life itself," because he knew the sound and the smell of her was the result of some miracle he'd brought about with the help of Geoff Yarrow, he was afraid of her as well, afraid of what he and Yarrow had done.

*

He was pretty sure that after it happened, he and Ann wouldn't have survived as a couple anyway. He found he couldn't bear to look at her and see his own grief reflected. The first time he'd slept with someone he met at a club, not telling her about Samantha, not telling her where he worked or even his name, he felt he had turned into someone else, and from that moment on he started to think about disappearing. When he came home the next morning Ann was dressing for work and did not even bother to ask where he'd been. It seemed stupid to him that they still did things like going to work, or grocery shopping, but they did, because what was the alternative? He wanted to find out.

Sleeping with nameless women he met in clubs hadn't torn them apart, though. Yarrow took care of that. The night Ann came home unexpectedly had done him in. When she walked into the bathroom and saw the viscera cooling in the tub. She freaked out like he'd just slaughtered somebody there, even though anybody could see it was just small animal parts. She said she didn't care. Said she was leaving.

"I only wanted to bring her back to us," he pleaded. "Yarrow and me, we were doing some— magick," the 'k' at the end of the word like an unfamiliar aftertaste. Yarrow always called it that: <u>magick</u>. Colin was sure that once Ann understood that she wouldn't be mad any longer. "You're sick." That was all she would say. That, and "Yarrow's sick too. I hate you both." She was frightened but wouldn't let him touch her. Later, of course, he realized she'd been right. It always went wrong in stories, after all, like that one, about the monkey's paw. He went to see Yarrow, to tell him to stop the experiments, that he'd changed his mind. The experiments had increasingly frightened him, anyway, even as they'd seem to embolden Yarrow. What had begun as a way out of his madness had come to seem like a harrowing path into something deeper. The last thing they'd done, the thing with the live rats that left the mess in the tub, had left him feeling sick and shaken for days.

Yarrow laughed, yellow teeth clacking behind thin lips, and said, "Too late, brother. It was always too late."

*

Yarrow said it wouldn't be like he was thinking. Not some dripping horror out of those old fifties comics. He said that bringing her back involved rending the very fabric of time and space. He said it casually, like he was talking about having another cup of coffee. It was the kind of thing Ann would have laughed at in different circumstances. She had no patience for metaphysical flights of fancy, for New Age speculation. Not that Yarrow embodied the daffy benevolence of a New Age guru. Yarrow was bad. Ann had said so the first time they'd met him, years ago, at a show at Berbati's. Colin couldn't remember the band that played but he remembered Yarrow sidling up to them and striking up a conversation and how Ann excused herself and didn't come back until Yarrow had gotten bored and moved on. "If I were a dog I could've smelled it on him," she said. "I'd growl at him if he walked into the room." Colin wondered how to tell her he'd given Yarrow their number and planned to hang out with him the next day. Yarrow had a great collection of 60s psychedelia on vinyl, he'd said, stuff you couldn't find anywhere nowadays, and they'd talked about Fantagraphics comics and Feral House books. Yarrow said he knew a guy that used to write for them. He was cool; Colin couldn't understand why Ann was being so weird about it all. Recently he'd looked back on the encounter and thought, did he deliberately pick us out? Was he planning to use us? Did he foresee it, or worse, did he make it happen? *Did my talking to Yarrow that night lead to everything that followed, to Samantha's conception and birth and her running in front of the car?* To the culmination of Yarrow's great experiment, at his expense, at the expense of them all. He'd considered the incident over and over, how Samantha's hand had slipped from his, how he'd let his attention wander for just a moment or two. Ann never said she blamed him. She never said much of anything, really. It would have been easier; he could have grown indignant and defended himself, convincing himself in the process that he was blameless.

Colin remembered how Yarrow had grinned at him the night he went to him following the bathtub debacle, those yellow teeth, the thin face and thin fingers and thin body racked by coughing fits only interrupted when he spoke or drew another drag off the hand-rolled cigarette that perpetually dangled from one hand. "I'm dying, too, you know," he said. "Not in that we're-all-dying bullshit way, but soon. Within a year, the doctor says. Think anybody'll care enough to bring me back?" Colin didn't answer. Not for the first time he wondered how old Yarrow might be: forty, or sixty, or more, or less. He had an agelessness about him that made him seem immortal. And, Colin thought: he looks just like a wolf. A lanky, starving, vicious wolf. He's going to eat me alive. Now. Colin said, "Help me."

*

Some tourists at the other end of the bar were talking to him. It took him a while to realize it. He wondered how they'd known he spoke English, but everywhere he went people seemed to know he didn't belong there. They moved down toward him with their drinks and soon the five of them were talking louder and louder and shrieking with unfunny laughter. One of the women was especially attractive,

The Moon Will Look Strange

with a strong profile that reminded him of Ann. He thought about trying to sleep with her but then pictured himself as he looked at that moment: seedy and drunk, alcohol and nicotine seeping from his pores. Maybe seedy and drunk was her type—you never knew—but he somehow doubted it. She and her friends were all American college students on a semester abroad and he saw in a flash his role in their story of this night. He was the weird and dissolute old guy, well past thirty, maybe even thirty-five. Once he realized this he started to play it up. Apparently seedy and drunk *was* her type. He couldn't remember what he'd said or done to close the deal or what path they took to the place where she was staying but somehow he was in her bed, she was under him and his cock felt harder than it ever had before and she was making noises that he guessed were pleasure, and then he came like all his life was pouring out of him into her. She was saying something but he couldn't hear her above the roaring in his ears. All at once it was a wolf's face he saw beneath him, and the grin stretching across yellowed teeth belonged to Yarrow. Yet her voice, not Yarrow's, reached him, and before he could understand he started telling her "sorry, sorry," because he figured he'd done something wrong, and she said it again, "You're hurting me."

"God, I'm sorry," he said again, and rolled off her. "It's okay," she said. She was waiting for him to say something else, he could tell, but he couldn't. She said, "God, that was fantastic" and when he didn't reply she flounced over onto one side. He felt bad, but lay quietly until it sounded like she'd stopped faking being asleep and really was, and he slipped out of her narrow bed and into the adjoining room. A clock blinked in a corner; it was not even midnight yet, though it felt very late indeed. He had a moment of panic fumbling with the unfamiliar lock, but saw the keys on a nearby table, and he let himself out.

He was relieved to find himself near the Plaza Nuevo and not lost in some part of town he didn't know. Tourists had warned him his first few days there that he'd be mugged in the Albaicín but he'd never had any problems; either he looked too disreputable to bother with or the danger was overstated. Now he fairly staggered along the cobblestone streets, still drunk although he'd felt fine back at the girl's place. He stopped to lean against the wall and shut his eyes while colors squirmed against his lids. Beer rose to the back of his throat and hung there, although he did not vomit. When he came to his senses again he was on his knees, still leaning with one hand against the wall, and he imagined he heard the sound of Yarrow's laughter ringing down the narrow stone pathway. But it was Samantha he smelled, Samantha fresh from her bath sweet with Johnson's Baby Shampoo and that soap Ann used to buy at Lush down on 23rd Avenue. He felt a sudden stab of homesickness, so unfamiliar he didn't know for a moment what to call it. Africa slipped away from him. He said, "I want to go home," and he was crying, just like that, he who had been the strong one throughout, who'd held Ann and his mother and his father and her parents as well through their sobbing. He wondered how he would get back there. He didn't have any money left, not enough for another plane ticket anyhow, but he longed for the alpine meadows

The Moon Will Look Strange

of Mount Hood, for a run along the river esplanade, even for a number 20 bus trundling down Burnside late at night, lurching with drunks and jittery with addicts. He cried, remembering. He put up his face to the night and howled like a dog and that felt better too. He still had friends, and family, and when he phoned them tomorrow they would send him money and he would go home again and they would put him back together somehow.

He never saw them coming. A blow to his back that knocked him flat—it didn't take much. He tried to pick himself up but couldn't. He didn't know how many of them there were but it felt like they were swarming him, like there were dozens. Hands reached into pockets, even his shoes, taking his wallet, his wristwatch. He felt something warm and liquid on his face and realized he was bleeding. He tried to talk to them although it took him several minutes for him to realize what he was saying to them. "Thank you." They were freeing him, once and for all. "Thank you," he said again. He stumbled to his feet and the moon swayed above him like the pendulum of a clock. He considered first that it was just as well he'd been unable to fight back, as he might have been seriously injured, and second that he seemed to have gotten drunker, more fucked-up since leaving the girl's apartment, as though the air itself was an intoxicant. Maybe he'd really been hurt. Maybe he'd hit his head when he fell, knocked himself out or something, but he couldn't feel a lump and the only blood came from his cut cheek.

So now he was free. He couldn't go home just yet. He'd get back to Tomas's, get his stuff and get out of there before dawn. He'd hitch down to the tip of Spain and he'd get to Morocco—"Shit," he said; he'd forgotten the ferries cost money. He'd figure something out once he got there. People always did. He had to move. Keep moving. That had been the problem. Keep moving till he got to someplace where she could cross over fully and find him. Once she did he'd get them both back to Ann somehow and she'd see, the three of them would be together again. She would see then how he'd fixed things, made everything right. He understood now why Yarrow had talked about rending the fabric of space and time. You had to tear the world apart to get back the thing that you loved. He stumbled and yelped and nearly fell. He'd imagined that something had reached out to trip him, but it was only a stray brick on the cobblestones.

"Help me," he'd said to Yarrow that day, but Yarrow had just sat back and laughed. "I already helped you," Yarrow said, "it's out of my hands." And maybe he was telling the truth: Yarrow was dead within a week of that visit. He'd been sicker than he'd let on. Colin had heard there would be a memorial service and went because he felt obligated. The ceremony had been held at a shabby home deep in north Portland, officiated by a young woman in thrift-store mourning wear, down to the black veil over an olive-skinned face, unadorned but for the tattooed spider under her left eye. Colin didn't recognize the handful of people in attendance and didn't speak to any of them, though each got up in turn and offered a halting and enigmatic appraisal of Yarrow as someone who had come to their aid in a time of despair. Something in the atmosphere was poisonous, unwholesome, and he slipped out the back before the affair was finished.

Next thing he knew he was in front of Tomas's, swaying in front of the massive wooden door. He couldn't remember how he'd gotten there, and he fumbled for his key, which somehow, blessedly, the thieves hadn't taken, maybe because he'd shoved it deep in the pocket of his jeans, maybe because they took pity on him at the last minute.

In the walled garden the detritus of the pond-cleaning lay scattered on the flagstones. The night was hot and dry yet he heard a splashing sound. The fish pond. They darted just below the surface of the now-clear water, bright and orange in the moonlight. Madih had set rocks about the pond, and built an island clear up to the surface. The fish swam in mad circles about the pond, beaching themselves on the rocks in pairs and threes and fours, their tails flicking madly at the surface of the water and one another, gills heaving, as they fought to thrust themselves back into the pond and then they repeated the same futile exercise over again. Colin watched them for a while. "Stupid," he said to them. "You're so stupid. No wonder you're fish, you're so stupid."

He wandered into his little room and stood in the middle, wondering why he'd bothered. He had a couple of items there, one or two cheap shirts he'd bought after arriving, a pair of shorts. Wasn't like he needed anything. He needed to get out. He tossed his key on the heavy wooden table and turned to leave.

Something made him turn back, a feeling, or something brushing against him perhaps. He couldn't help it. "Samantha?" Her name felt like something dead in his mouth. He couldn't smell her any longer like he had before. Something waited for him in the room that was both Samantha and not Samantha any longer. He took a deep breath. He had to be brave for the both of them. Of course she would be changed by her experience. She would be frightened when she came back, she wouldn't understand what had happened to him, to either of them, and he had to stay strong.

"It's okay, baby," he murmured. "It's going to be okay." Back out, past the doomed fish in the pond, through the doors again and onto the street. She was almost corporeal. He was sure of it. "Come on," he said. He climbed the stone steps, brushing the wall with his fingertips to steady himself. The moon had grown so brilliant it hurt his eyes. He wished all at once that Ann could be with him right now. He imagined what her face would look like when she saw Samantha again. Or maybe it wouldn't be like that at all. Maybe it would be like none of it had ever happened. That would be best, he thought. Otherwise it would be so difficult to explain to people. He wished he had asked Yarrow for more details, how he should act, what they should do.

He was breathing heavily, as though he'd been running a great distance. The stairs were steep and many, but they shouldn't have put him out of breath like this. Yarrow's voice repeated like a loop inside his head: the moon will look strange the moon will look strange the moon will look strange. And he threw his head back and it did look strange, enormous and somehow pregnant, its deep malignant orange

The Moon Will Look Strange

saturating the sky. Yarrow had said, this is how you will know. And here round the corner the sky was vast and the town stretched below him and across the canyon the Alhambra flamed, aglow in the miraculous light of this new and different moon. People gathered like wraiths along the wall, milling about and pointing and asking one another questions, but he couldn't understand what they were saying. Tourists on a night visit to the Alhambra amassed on the ramparts, tiny faraway figures. He could hear their cries. It's okay, Samantha, he told her, whether with speech or in his heart he could not be certain. It's okay, people are frightened and you are frightened, but soon everything will be all right again. Everything will be the way it ought to be.

His skin prickled, the back of his neck and along his arms. He swung round, crouching to embrace her, and lost his balance, catching himself with one hand on the cobblestones, an unfortunate recovery as his hand came away covered in dog shit. Something was wrong. "Samantha?" he said, and he heard his voice hoarse and raw with panic. Someone answered him. Someone said, "Thank you, Colin," but Samantha didn't call him Colin, she called him Daddy, and what stepped from the shadows wasn't a little girl but a grown man, yellow teeth bright in the moonlight, his face like a wolf's. He shimmered in the unnatural light, like he wasn't yet real. The moon was full to bursting now, bright as the sun, and some of the weeping people along the wall seemed to be praying. Colin saw a man hoist himself up on the side, shouting something, tears streaming down his face before hurling himself over and into the canyon on the other side. "You did well," Yarrow said, "you did exactly as I asked you. You did every single thing." Colin, still not understanding, reached for him, reached for something but Yarrow sidestepped him, laughing, and gravelly, mocking, said, "This is the way the world ends. This is the way the world ends and a new one begins. She's not coming back, Colin. She never was." Ann voice: *If I were a dog I could have smelled it on him*. Colin remembered his earlier conviction, that Yarrow had set the whole thing in motion the night they'd met for the first time. He pleaded, because there was nothing left to do. "What's going to happen? What happens next? What did you make me do?" Yarrow only laughed and shrugged, and Colin saw now that in a matter of minutes he'd become horribly solid and realer, realer than anything else about him. "I don't know what happens next," Yarrow admitted. "No one's ever done anything like this before." Colin shut his eyes but even then the moon grew bigger and brighter behind his eyelids, and he felt the world shift and change, shaping itself into something new, something he didn't know, something that didn't exist before, and there was only the moon and the void and Yarrow's voice low and incantatory: *oh the moon oh the moon yes the moon will look strange*.

The Moon Will Look Strange

In Death's Other Kingdom

She is back again, this woman who wears my face. I hid in the walls to spy on her. I hid in the floorboards and felt her soles pressing down on me. She says I am a ghost in the house but it is she who is the ghost, the ghost of the present, the ghost of the future, the ghost of what will never be.

Listen: wherever it is that I am, this much I know: I am *not* dead.

*

I met Richard in the dog park. I was two months out from a disastrous engagement and walking my best friend Corin's dog Daisy on a daily basis to force myself out of my studio apartment so I didn't succumb to the despair of the unloved, unemployed, unanchored. I was too depressed to do anything else. Dust bunnies and silence were my constant companions. I'd moved out of my ex-fiance's place in a hurry and couldn't be bothered to unpack in the dismal room where I'd landed. Books, comics, zines, my beloved vintage vinyl (I had nothing to play it on) languished in stacks on the floor next to boxes I'd only rummage through when I needed something out of them: a coffee cup, a clean sweater, different drawing pencils.

Lynda E. Rucker

I don't even like dogs really. Of course, I pretended I did.

We sized each other up for a couple of days before he introduced himself to me and asked me if I wanted to get a cup of coffee with him. He had an easy confidence about him that I liked. After that, you know the story. We fell into bed, fell in love, roughly in that order—at least I did; he cared about me, certainly, but I don't know if he is actually capable of falling in love.

My inability to unpack turned out to be a boon as it made moving into his place much easier. I left the dust bunnies behind without regret along with the studio where I'd been convinced mere weeks earlier that I'd die a lonely death, eaten by cockroaches.

He was everything a man is not supposed to be to the modern woman in this day and age. He was the one who made everything okay again. He was, in the words of my long-abandoned religious childhood (I won't get into it, but let's just say my parents would give Carrie's mom a run for her money), my alpha and omega, my beginning and my end.

He was going to look after me. Why look for a stupid minimum wage job, he said; I needed to focus on my art. He made enough for the both of us. The work I did mattered.

When I was with him, I knew everything was going to be okay.

*

I suppose an introduction is in order, although I always liked that poem by Emily Dickinson: *I'm*

The Moon Will Look Strange

nobody! Who are you? But since it isn't acceptable to be nobody, since it seems we must: I'm Grace. I'm an artist. I drew and wrote the comic strip "Beverly" for the local alternarag. Beverly was like – well, remember those Emily the Strange books? Imagine if Emily grew up and went really, really bad and ended up in a strip by Roberta Gregory, the creator of Bitchy Bitch. It's hard to explain really. You sort of had to be there with Beverly to get it. But it was sort of gothy and sort of surreal and very satirical and quite vulgar and, I thought, funny. Other people agreed; it was popular around town. My ambition was to write and draw comics for a living one day and not just for beer money. (Why am I speaking of myself in the past tense? Just wait. We're getting to that.)

What's in a name, anyway? Richard's name, it doesn't suit him. It's too formal. It's to something. Or maybe it suits him exactly because it lies about who he is and he is a man made of lies from head to toe. I never knew anyone who could lie so blatantly, so unblinkingly, so *truthfully*.

At first, I believed him to be the stable core to my artistic flights of fancy. He taught philosophy at the university. He made a good-to-me salary and owned a beautiful but not bourgeoisie home. I know; you are picturing a circle of adoring undergraduate girls around him. But that didn't worry me; I wasn't *the jealous type*. I knew he'd made his choice, and he only wanted me.

Because he did, of course, have a reputation, before he met me. His friends made jokes about it; women sent knowing glances in his direction. And sometimes drinks, or offers of more. He assured me he'd put all that behind him.

Corin took me out one night just before I moved in with him and asked me if I knew what I was doing. If I was sure. If this wasn't just some rebound thing. If he was really going to make me happy. Of course he was, I assured her.

You know how that goes. Our relationship is special in a way that no one can possibly understand. Nobody else gets *us*, that's what you think. I didn't really see Corin much after that. Relationships alter friendships sometimes and Corin drifted away from me, as did the handful of other people I'd had in my life up to that point.

We were different. I wasn't some timid housewife. I was a cool girl. People had crushes on *me*, thought Richard was lucky to have landed me. I loved sex. I was up for anything. I was *fun*.

It wasn't enough.

With men like Richard, it never is.

*

Exhibit A: It's been one week since we moved in together. I am, as you'll remember, gainfully unemployed, and it's spring break, so we're binging on TV series on DVD. I don't even remember which ones, *Buffy* or *Mad Men* or *The Wire* or *Breaking Bad*, whether they were old or new or even if we're enjoying them. It doesn't matter, you see – I'm just so happy to be with Richard, to have fallen in love again so quickly when I thought my heart would be iced over forever. His dog, Wendall, the dog who introduced us, as we liked to tell people, is snuffling between us on the sofa.

Wait, let's back up one more time. Because otherwise you have no way of understanding *why* I was so in love with him. Here: he talked to me about my comics and the art I made like they were something real and good, and he was the first person who really made me believe in myself. My ex-fiancé had always treated my work like a slightly embarrassing hobby I'd give up on once I started breeding or whatever. Also, Richard was really practical, and I am not. And the sex was amazing. That probably accounted for more of it than I'd want to admit. I thought that meant something, that the fact that from the first time he ran his hands over my body he seemed to know exactly what I needed better than I knew myself was some sort of indication we were meant to be together. Really, all it meant was that he was great in bed.

He listened to my dreams and he made himself a part of them—no, he did more than that. He became my future. He fit into my life like he'd always been there. I could no longer envision a *me* without *him*.

So anyway, here we are in exhibit A, framed in the living room window of Richard's fashionably rickety hundred year old house with a flickering TV light setting us all aglow and we're laughing and talking and sharing a ridiculously expensive bottle of wine—oh, he used to spend too much money on me, that made me feel special as well.

It took me a while to notice as we sat there that night that he kept replying to text messages. But eventually I did, and I found it annoying that someone or someones were interfering with our little idyll, and said so, and he said too much, something about a student panicking over a paper due at the end of the break. And even then, I didn't stop to think it was weird: a student with a professor's personal cell phone number, texting repeatedly after midnight during a vacation. I know it sounds ridiculous, but that's how implicitly I trusted him.

The other thing I remember about that night is that I got up once to use the bathroom and when I came back, I scared myself; it was just my reflection in the window, a translucent me looking like a ghost already.

*

Something very frightening is happening. I'm finding these pages, but I didn't write them. The story they are telling is not true. Or rather, it's partly true, but it's altered, it isn't my story, it's not the way things are.

I couldn't have written them, and I must have written them—because they are in my handwriting, but they are not my words and they are not my story.

*

I didn't think it would be so dark in this place, wherever it is. I suppose I never thought of this place at all, though. Is it limbo? Is it purgatory?

One thing I need to make clear. When I say she is wearing my face, it's not a metaphor. Nor is this the document of a dissociated madwoman. Would that it was: insanity would provide spells of relief. There is none of that here. My chest is forever tight with unshed tears.

Why don't I shed them, then? I can't cry any longer. I don't have the means. I can't—I don't quite know where I am, you see, or what I am, what is left of me. And wisps of me disappear from the house each passing day. Sometimes she leaves with parts of me and doesn't bring them back, like my grandmother's scarf or my favorite sketchbook.

I know that time has passed because they both came in the other day and they were laughing and snowflakes powdered their hair and coats. Somehow what made me especially sad about it was that it seemed I'd missed autumn, my favorite season. Formerly my favorite season. In the place I've gone to, I don't know if I'm allowed to have season. Or favorites.

You wonder where I've gone to. Am I sure I'm not dead, you might be wondering? I don't know. Maybe I'm wrong. What do you think? And if I am, what should I do? You think you'd know what to do when you are dead, but I don't. I don't know where to go, or more to the point, I don't seem to be able to go anywhere else, so I hang around here. Is this what a ghost is?

No, I don't think I'm dead. It seems worse than that somehow.

*

Exhibit B: I am in love, but I am not entirely deluded. It does not take a terribly long time for the text messaging and other behaviors too tedious and predictable to recount to create suspicion even in me. You know how this sordid story goes: I snoop, I read a few incriminating texts, I cry and accuse, he fobs me off with stories of obsessed girls with overactive imaginations and dalliances who can't seem to let go now he's become respectable with me. His excuses don't go very far, and soon I am weeping at my drawing table and missing deadlines and thinking of the studio with the dust bunnies and the silence and wondering if that's just my lot in life, my fate, a lonely dwindling of dreams in a forgotten room.

Then there came a moment that thrust me out of my pathetic inertia. We were out at a gig, and it was a hot night, and I'd stepped outside for some air and a smoke and I turned to go in and—

They weren't even trying to hide. A man and a woman in an alleyway next to the club and they were kissing each other, he had his hand on the back of her head in a familiar way and I felt like I might catch fire, the rage in me was so intense. At myself, at him, at the random girl, at the sordidness and patheticness of it all. *How dare he.* I was trembling all over.

I didn't do anything though. I went back in the club. I pretended I hadn't seen anything. Later the girl smirked at me from across the room. *The stupid, clueless wife.*

I gazed back at her coolly. Already my heart was turning to stone.

By the way, this is not the story of a woman scorned. It's fair at this point to confess that I have, as they say, buried the lede.

The Moon Will Look Strange

*

No. No. No. This is not the way it happened at all.

I am gathering these pages, I am burning them all. All of them lies.

*

Here we go with the childhood thing. I said I would not get into this. I was wrong. How could I not?

My parents were what used to be called holy rollers—Southern Pentecostal Holiness, to be exact, and they brought me up to be like them, speaking in tongue and getting taken by the spirit and having personal conversations with Jesus himself like he was some kind of therapist.

I was maybe ten or eleven when I was talking to some of my little Pentecostal girlfriends and it started to occur to me that the Jesus I was talking to and the conversations I was having were not quite the same as their experiences.

You see, my Jesus was a lot more—*real* than their Jesus.

I said this isn't the story of a woman scorned. It's also not the story of how I lost my faith. Faith I have in bucketloads. Faith I have too much of. I know there's more to heaven and earth. I've seen it. I've spoken with it.

I've whispered my deepest secrets in its ear late at night.

Lynda E. Rucker

So then I did what every little girl ought to be able to do when she starts suspecting that maybe it's not Jesus she's talking to, but the *other one*, the enemy, the prince of lies. (That's what I began to call Richard in my head, you know. The Prince of Lies.)

I was a little bit proud, to be honest. After all, if the devil was coming especially to me and trying to trick *me*, I must be pretty important.

My mother said I was making things up. She said the things I reported weren't real. Said I was a bad, evil little girl. Said I was sent to test her.

Things were never the same after that. My parents thought I was some kind of abomination. He became my only ally in the world. My confidante, my friend. He was very handsome—you see, that's why I thought he was Jesus. But as childhood slipped away and puberty set in my senses sharpened. I detected a rank smell of decay on his flesh and when he spoke to me, sitting by my window in the moonlight as he always did, a strange hissing sound wended its way under his words, a language ancient and terrible. His skin that had looked so smooth and unblemished to me as a child was thick and scaly and peeling off in places.

I had entrusted all my truths to him, the light and the dark. He knew me inside and out, my strengths and weaknesses, what made me happy and what made me ashamed. After all, I'd thought he was Jesus, and I had no one to listen to me—so I went right on talking.

The Moon Will Look Strange

I had figured out by then that if he wasn't Jesus, he wasn't the devil either; neither of them existed, stand-ins for things older and stranger and harder to understand. I told him to go away and leave me alone but he wouldn't. Between the thing in my room at night and my parents praying for me all through the day, my adolescent home life was more challenging than most, and school doesn't even bear mentioning. I opted for many a troubled teen's time-honored solution and ran away from home.

*

Which brings me to now. Did I skip over some bits? Yes, that was purposeful. I don't like to remember those years. Oh, very well, it isn't what you're thinking. I didn't end up raped, abused, forced into prostitution, and addicted to drugs.

You see, I ran away from home and the very thing I ran away from followed me.

I couldn't get away from him. Sleeping under a bridge somewhere: I open my eyes, he's there, talking to me. He started turning up in the daytime, too, like when I'd board a city bus to get away from bad weather and he'd join me, sitting beside me, always whispering at me.

He was everywhere.

So I did what I had to do. I made the best of a bad situation. I had him fix things for me.

And he did. I landed on my feet; I got a caseworker, got emancipated, got an apartment, got a job, got a GED, got accepted to art school. All my efforts to shed him had been for naught, but as I edged out of my teen years into adulthood, he became less of a presence, and the space between his visits grew longer. Eventually, I convinced myself he'd been a childhood imagining. A hallucination born of desperation. An isolated psychosis.

Even as I believed this, I filled sketchbooks with images of him, like I could draw him down to his essence, solve the puzzle of who he had been and why he had come to me at all.

After he left me alone, I didn't know whether to be relieved or bereft. I'd never been so alone, and even if the thing that had kept me company throughout my life had been some kind of demon, well, it was better than being lonely. It's probably the reason that afterward I kept hooking up with the worst types of men. Better the devil you know.

The devil I knew. He came back to me that night in the club. At first I only smelled him. Not elsewhere, but on me. *In* me. His rankness seeped from my sweat glands and tainted my saliva. I tried to tell him in my head: *Go away, I don't want you here anymore. I never wanted you here.*

But he'd never listened to me.

In the bathroom at the club, I stared at myself under the stupid black lights, and I thought I could see him hiding behind my eyes and I said *How did you get in here?* and he wouldn't answer me.

I threw up twice in the toilet and then I left the club without telling anyone and hailed a cab.

*

"Baby, where did you go? I was so worried

about you."

Smelling of wine and weed, Richard nuzzled me and I thrust myself away from him. "I'm getting sick," I mumbled. "I'm going to sleep on the couch." He was saying something to me as I tromped out of the room we shared. I didn't even care about what had happened with him and that random girl at the club; I was too busy being panicked about the return of that *thing*. How do you bring up something like that? "Darling, I forgot to mention—I'm possessed."

The following morning I was a little hurt that he didn't check on me on the couch before he left for campus. Alone in the house, I examined myself. I was in a very bad way. My arms and legs, my breasts, my torso, all of me was covered in weeping black sores, like I was rotting from within. I knew what had happened; somehow, that thing had gotten *in* me, and my mortal flesh was being consumed by it. Soon there would be nothing left of me.

I did what every girl does when she's at the end of her rope. I called my mother.

*

It wasn't that straightforward, of course. I hadn't spoken to either of my parents in more than ten years, and at first I had to go through an aunt who'd grudgingly acted as a go-between at crucial points, but she had to take me on the full-service guilt tour before she'd give out any contact information. Meanwhile my teeth were turning to jelly in my jaw and my tongue was swelling and blackening by the minute. I finally got off the line with her and dialed my mother's number.

I burst into tears when I heard her voice. Isn't that funny? Everything she'd done to me, all the ways she'd abandoned me, and yet.

She said, "Why are you calling me?"

I tried to tell her. I tried to tell her that he was back and consuming me even as we spoke, but he'd taken my voice. When I started to speak, I sounded like *him*.

"Is this some kind of joke? Who is this?" she said, and then she hung up.

The phone slipped from my hand. I couldn't hold it any longer because my fingers had gone limp and boneless.

Despite what he'd done to me, I couldn't stop thinking about Richard, what he would find when he got home, what he would think, how it would devastate him.

Somehow I made my way back into the bedroom. And that's when I saw it—saw myself, I mean, sleeping on the bed, clothes rumpled around me. I reached out to touch her and as I did so my arm passed before the window and the sunlight and the dust motes fell through it.

I was no more.

*

In this place, time does not move in a linear fashion, but I do have a lot of it. Plenty of time to think, since I can't do much else—think, and observe. And I've been thinking about the demon, and how it came to me. Where did it come from? Why me?

The Moon Will Look Strange

People may laugh at the kind of Christian community I came out of, and the even more radical fringes like the snake-handlers or the sorts of people who nail themselves to crosses for Easter. The true believers. We see them and we think: ridiculous, backward, superstitious, deluded.

But just because you've gotten the names and the stories wrong doesn't mean you can't touch the numinous.

So what I have come to believe is that at a very young age, too young to resist or understand what was happening, I let something in. I think this happens to young children all the time. Those monsters in the closet, or under the bed? They're all real. And kids see them for what they are, and they banish them—children frightened of sinister shapes in the night have far more power than they realize. But because I didn't recognize my monster for what it was, it got stronger and stronger.

I think it's been trying to get back to me ever since I was able to banish it once I finally grew up. If they can trick us for long enough, these monsters, the tastes of life that they take from us must be so sweet.

Its transformation into me has not been exact. Most importantly, she cannot draw like me. To hide this, she quit drawing at all. She told Richard she was done, and that she wanted to have a family with him.

To his credit, he balked at that: was she sure? She knew that he didn't expect such a thing of her, didn't she? I don't think she understood that it didn't please him, but he accepted it in the end—after all, wasn't it what she wanted?

When he is not at home she talks to me. She says she knows I am still lingering. She says I am a ghost, but as I asked you at the beginning of all this, how can I be a ghost if I'm not dead?

I notice how Richard touches her, how he looks at her. He knows something is not right. He gets a speculative expression on his face. Then it passes, because what else could he think? Anything else is madness.

He keeps his girls, a steady stream of nubile sexual variety to hand, and she keeps the house. This seems to be working out well for everyone involved except me.

*

A terrible thing has happened.

They came in today with two little girls, identical twins, maybe six or so. At first I thought they must be children of friends, that perhaps they were babysitting—but then I realized.

I've been trapped in this place so much longer than I realized. They were her—its—children, its and Richard's.

Because it looks like me, *they* look like me.

Because they belong to *it*, I wonder if there is a blankness in their eyes, and a smell about their flesh, but I cannot bear to examine them too closely. They are only children, after all.

But so much time has passed. I had no idea.

I have to do more. So I start in small ways. There is still much of *me* in *her*.

The Moon Will Look Strange

She chooses tea instead of coffee for breakfast. She doesn't know why. Her hand simply moved that way, reached for the kettle and the tea bag rather than the coffeemaker.

She reaches out to touch one of the girls, and touches the other.

She reaches out to touch Richard, and her hand falls short.

The distance between them grows.

She suspects me, but she's weakened by her mortal form. She can't touch me here. She can only rage at me, and rage she does when is alone in the house. Anyone would take her for a madwoman.

*

The girls must be ten or eleven now. It's of no concern to me. I've had a triumph. She has just woken from a kind of fugue. She's filled three pages on a legal pad with sketches. My sketches. Old Beverly, up to her old tricks again. They're funny, and they're clever, just like I used to be.

I sense that so much time in my form is changing her. She is forgetting what she is. She truly believes herself to *be* me. She doesn't rage at me so much any longer because my existence is becoming like a bad dream to her. A bad dream she had about a woman who haunted her, a woman who used to be here, who wore her face. It is so strange, and she even tries to tell Richard about it once, but they don't talk much anymore.

She doesn't understand why the sketches upset her so much. She destroys them, but I just make more of them. I fill page after page. She buys pencils and sketch pads without knowing why. I am producing art on a prodigious scale. She can't destroy my work fast enough. She gives up. She puts it away. She tries to believe it's coming from her. She can't.

I'm coming back, and she knows it.

*

No. This is not the way it happened, is happening. There is only one Prince of Lies, and that's the one who has penned most of this story.

*

The girls are teenagers now. They remind me of myself. Still identical, but different from one another. The smaller, slighter one is also mouthier, more rebellious. She's going to be trouble. The other one is more studious. She's not yet learned that toeing the line brings you no rewards in the end. I can never remember their names. Their names don't matter to me.

She's reading this now. She's found it. She wrote it all down. I made her. She's reading this sentence right now, and she thinks she's going mad, but she isn't.

It's worse than that: she's going to cease to exist. Or she's going back to this place I am in. It doesn't matter which: it's all the same.

She's hysterical now because she doesn't remember anything any longer. She believes that she's the one who belongs here. She believes that she

The Moon Will Look Strange

defeated me to reclaim her rightful place in the world among the living. She begs me not to do this. For the sake of her children. For the sake of her family. As if I would harm any of them. As if they are not also blood of my blood, flesh of my flesh.

To be honest, I'm no longer sure now. Which of us is real and which is the demon?

I don't care any longer. *I've come back.*

Someone's at the door. Richard is home early. I hear him say my name, and he's talking to me as he walks through the house, but I don't really notice what he's saying. I'm so happy to be home again. Back to *my* family. Back to *my* life.

But he walks across the threshold into the kitchen and the instant he sees me, his face changes. I say, "Darling." I open my arms. They're *my arms* again. But his expression is one of horror. He's reeling away from me. Why? I've done nothing wrong. I've only tried to come back to the place where I belong. I pick up my drawings, I thrust them at him. "Look," I say to him. "It's me, it's Grace. I came back to you. It took years and years, but I came back to you at last."

He is looking at me like am some kind of monster, some kind of *thing*. His mouth is forming words he cannot seem to utter, and the drawings spill from my hands and across the floor, and the chasm between us is endless.

Lynda E. Rucker

Ash-Mouth

In the long and terrible summer of Ivy's eleventh year, the summer she spent smiling with her mouth closed because she was still losing her baby teeth (she suffered from a socially lethal combination of being both too small and too smart for her age), the summer she itched and sweated through a cast on her arm acquired not a week after school ended (she broke it falling off the porch at her Nana's house), the summer her sister Holly went missing, the summer something called *Ash-Mouth* crept into Ivy's nightmares and crouched in the shadows of her waking life like one of the furies in her *Children's Encyclopedia of Greek Myths*, that same summer, a black and white kitten turned up in her backyard with a dead lizard in its mouth and a feral glint in its eyes. Ivy's mother pitched a fit when she caught her daughter feeding it dinner scraps, saying she could barely make ends meet as it was without worrying about paying for vet bills and cat food, but then Holly disappeared and nothing more was said about what Ivy was and wasn't allowed to do.

Ivy's Nana suggested a name for it, Chiaroscuro, shortened to Kiki because no one could pronounce or remember it and anyway, Nana said, it was a special word: not ordinary, an artists' word, which made it an enchanted word, a word about the contrast between black and white, light and dark.

The Moon Will Look Strange

Nobody, Nana said, nobody was all one or all the other, even if they tried to tell you different, and the most magical place of all was the place where light met dark; but that was a great secret.

Why? Why is that a secret? Ivy, ever-inquisitive, had to know.

Nana said, *I'll tell you when you're older*, but she never did, and the years passed and Kiki turned into a cat, grew old and died, and Ash-Mouth faded into the epoch of childhood dread, and Holly never came home. Twenty-five years later, Ivy, easing her car to the curb in front of Nana's little white bungalow, boxing herself between a red pickup truck with a Jesus fish on the bumper and a bright yellow VW Beetle, found herself looking at her hands, looking at the Beetle in her rearview window, looking at everything she could think of to look at that was not Nana's house, and not knowing why.

It was dusk, and the eaves did not seem to extend far enough to cast such long dark shadows, and yet they did; and why did the dark sit in squat dense patches round the shrubbery? Ivy hurried up the walkway and rapped on Nana's door, telling herself it was only the chill of late autumn that made her anxious to get inside. The door swung in and Nana peered round it, blinking. Her healthy color was gone, her face drawn and pale, her hair oily and yellow-looking.

Ivy, she's saying someone is following her from room to room. I can't talk to her. Can you go see?

"Oh!" said Nana. "Was it today you were coming?" and opened up the door a little more so Ivy could step past her into the gloom of the narrow hallway. It was just as cold inside as out, and it smelled, though Ivy couldn't say what it reminded her of. The sounds of a cheering studio audience drifted down joylessly from the television in the living room. "Did you drive all the way here in one day? What about your job?"

"I'm visiting Mom, remember?" Ivy leaned to kiss her grandmother on the cheek. "And I'm on sabbatical, anyway. I told you that." She saw that the word meant nothing to her grandmother. "I'm not doing any teaching right now, just research."

"That's right. I remember," and Nana nodded, even though she didn't. "I know it's not good how things come and go. Your mother gets so angry at me when it happens! She's very irritable, isn't she?"

"I don't know," Ivy said. "She said you'd been having some trouble."

"I saw you on that television program!" Nana exclaimed. "The one with all the scientists. I couldn't understand a thing you folks were talking about, except that it was something to do with outer space."

She was dissembling. "I'm a scientist now, too, Nana. I'm glad you got to see it. I can get you a tape of it if you want. But let's talk about why I'm here."

"You'll want some coffee," Nana said. Ivy followed her into the kitchen, where an ancient percolator wheezed and hissed on the stove. The room itself was cheerless, the bare bulb in the ceiling inadequate to dispel the gloom.

"It's awfully cold in here, Nana. You're not having trouble with the heating, are you?"

The Moon Will Look Strange

"It's always something." Nana shook her head as she filled two mugs and passed one to Ivy. "The man came to look at it and he said he didn't see a problem."

"Well, do you want me to put another light bulb in here for you?" Ivy took one sip of her coffee and set it down; it tasted old, and her mouth was gritty with grounds.

"I'm not helpless. I know your mother made it sound that way, but I'm not. She never believes a word I say." Nana leaned in closer. "I know she comes here, looking for me. She gets in at night and she prowls the walls and the ceiling. And sometimes I can hear her in the pipes."

"Who? Who's getting in here?"

Nana whispered it. "Ash-Mouth."

*

It had been Holly's idea.

"I don't want to," Ivy had said.

"Scaredy-cat." Holly's eyes got narrow and mean. "Chickenshit." They were sitting across from one another in a booth at the Mini-Burger, eating corndogs.

"I heard that," Big Ray said from behind the counter. "You don't be talking to your little sister that way." Big Ray was always scolding you like you were one of his own, even though his kids had all been grown up forever. He'd run the Mini-Burger for as long as the girls had been alive, maybe the whole forty years it had been open. When the owner had died a couple of summers back, his son had come down from Atlanta and tried to "update" the menu. According to Ray, "We run that Yankee on back out of town so fast he didn't know what hit him."

"Atlanta ain't Yankee," Holly had whispered to Ivy when Big Ray told them this story.

"It is to Big Ray," Ivy had whispered back. "Don't say ain't."

Just then, Holly was ignoring Big Ray. "When school starts back, I'm telling everyone you're scared of *everything*."

That was how it had started, and so it was all Holly's fault, and she ought to leave, that was what she ought to do; it was Holly's fault and nobody else's that she hadn't come out of the culvert after scaring Ivy the way she did, scaring her screaming out onto the flat dead-grass lots of Milltown. Behind her, the big concrete drainage pipe cut into the hillside, and above it ran a disused railway track that had once carried passengers, then freight, then nothing at all. The opening of the pipe looked ragged and wounded with branches from above hanging down over it. All around her, the vacant lots where kids went to drink and get high on weekends were littered with crushed beer cans, cigarette butts, the occasional spent condom. Ivy kicked at an empty vodka bottle. It was hot, her arm itched under her cast, and she wanted to go home.

All Holly's fault. *If we find Ash-Mouth, maybe she won't take Nana away.*

Ash-Mouth came for you when you died, according to Nana. She knew this because when she was a little girl, her cousin had died of polio, and she had seen Ash-Mouth steal into his room on the night

The Moon Will Look Strange

he died. Nana had described Ash-Mouth to them. She had bone-colored hair, and a sludgy-looking smoke trailed from her fingertips. Her hair gave off sparks. In place of a heart, she had a piece of coal burning at the center of her chest, and her teeth—which were very sharp—were made up of diamonds brought up from the core of the earth, where monsters still lived. Her mouth itself was the yawning maw of a grave; her breath stunk like a crematorium: burning flesh, cold damp ashes, and death.

I bet there's no such thing Holly had whispered in Ivy's ear the first time Nana told them about Ash-Mouth, but Ivy knew better, because she could close her eyes and picture her just the way Nana described her. So it was easy enough for Holly to talk about looking for Ash-Mouth when she only half-believed in it, if that much. She had been like that all summer: bossy and *insufferable*, a word Ivy had learned in the school spelling bee. Holly was insufferable because Ivy was what her parents called precocious, and due to that precociousness she was going to skip right over the sixth grade and move up to the junior high with Holly. Holly wasn't happy with this arrangement. Their parents argued about it, but their parents argued about everything. Ivy had stood in the doorway of the kitchen watching them fight, and they were so angry at one another they never even noticed her there.

Ivy's father said it wasn't good for either one of the girls. "What are we supposed to do, then?" their mother had said. "Ivy's bored to tears, and it's not like this town has a private school, even if we could afford one." That wasn't strictly true; there was a Christian school operating out of Bethel Holiness Church where about fifty kids (all of them white) made up the entire student body, K-12, but Ivy didn't think that was the kind of private education her mother meant. She went on, "We're not going to handicap Ivy just to save Holly's feelings."

Ivy was ashamed to be the source of so much trouble between her parents and her sister. She resolved then that she would try to do worse in school, but when the time came the test or the homework assignment was always so babyish she couldn't pretend it wasn't effortless. Anyway, Ivy planned to be an astronaut when she grew up. She didn't have that kind of time to waste, not even when the kids called her that name, *Poison Ivy*, not even when Brandi Henderson, who was big and mean, grabbed her in the bathroom and said Ivy better let her copy off her test paper or she'd stick her head in the toilet. Ivy kept her tests carefully covered after that, and avoided the bathroom at all costs, even if it meant eating and drinking nothing at all from the time she woke up in the morning until she got home from school.

At the junior high, at least, she wouldn't have Brandi to worry about. With any luck, Brandi would never make it past sixth grade.

"Hey," someone said behind her, and she jumped, but it was only Greg, a boy who lived over in Milltown, a boy who was a grade ahead of Holly in school. Holly had a crush on him.

"Hey," Greg said again, "what are you doing?"

He was wearing a white muscle shirt and blue

shorts that hung down to his knees. Grownups didn't like Greg. Ivy and Holly's father had told them to stay away from Milltown altogether—because it was full of drunks and addicts and poor white trash—and Greg in particular—because his brother Rusty was mixed up with some Mexican drug dealers and his father had done time in prison. But *their* father had moved out of the house at the beginning of the summer, a betrayal so acute that nothing he said could hold sway over them any longer.

"Where's your sister?" Greg asked.

"I don't know," Ivy said. "She went in there," pointing at the culvert.

"What'd she do that for?"

"We were playing a game," Ivy said, vague. "I think she's trying to scare me. She's hiding somewhere. Playing a trick on me." Ivy hoped that this would turn out to be true.

Greg grinned. "We should play one back at her."

"We shouldn't," Ivy said. "We should tell her to get on out of there right now."

*

Nana had gotten sick at the beginning of the summer, right after Ivy broke her arm, and since then she had been in and out of the hospital for something the girls' mother wouldn't talk to them about. She was the last of their grandparents, indeed, the only one they'd ever known. People said her husband, their grandfather, had just up and disappeared one day, but Nana had told Holly and Ivy that wasn't true. What had happened was that Nana woke up in the morning and realized he hadn't come to bed the night before. She went downstairs to look for him and all she found was a pile of ashes in the seat of his favorite leather chair, a singed spot on the arm, and one shoe.

"He burned himself *up*?" Ivy said in amazement.

It looked like he had just caught on fire, but how could that happen without anything else burning up too? Nana cleaned up what she could. It was only one of many strange things that happened to Nana in her lifetime, and she hadn't liked him much by then anyway, so she took it in her stride. But for the rest of her life she kept half-expecting that he'd come through the door, and she was scared people would say she'd done away with him. Years later she read a book about other, similar cases, and when she told Holly and Ivy the story she showed them a picture from the book: spontaneous human combustion, the caption read, and below it a hard-to-make-out photo that the text beneath explained was a shot of the unblemished kitchen where a woman had gone up in flames before the shocked eyes of her family.

Nana told them other stories, too, frightening, extraordinary stories. *When I was a little girl*, Nana said, *I didn't realize the stories in books were made up. I thought they were true.*

That had confused Ivy. All stories in books were made up, but that didn't mean they weren't true.

I have always seen ghosts hovering round. It took me half my life to learn to hold my tongue until I was sure whatever I was looking at was bound to this earth.

The Moon Will Look Strange

Nana's family had been very religious, and had tried to cast the devil out of her when she was a little girl. Later on she spent time in a mental hospital (*we don't call them insane asylums*, the girls' mother would tell them, her mouth tight, when she overheard them talking about it, *and anyway, Mother's not to be telling you stories like that*). Nana said they had drilled electricity right into her brain; Ivy pictured her with all her hair standing on end and lightning shooting out of her ears.

They'll do that to you *if they find out how weird you are* Holly had said to her.

So she wouldn't tell Greg what she had seen in the culvert before she lost Holly, down in the earth in the deep dark.

*

"It's dangerous in there, you know," Greg said. "Kids go in and they don't come out the other side. Happens all the time."

"It does?"

He laughed. "Naw, it ain't even that long. I been through it a million times. I bet Holly's on the other side, waiting to scare you."

"No," said Ivy, "she didn't go out the other end."

"Come on," Greg said. "I'll go with you. There's nothing to be scared of, you'll see."

The only thing worse than going back in there was waiting while somebody else went in and maybe didn't come out the other side. She didn't know what she'd do if that happened, so she followed Greg.

Lynda E. Rucker

Just inside the culvert, spray-painted names and obscenities and declarations of 4-ever love covered the concrete. At other times of year a wash ran down the middle but the summer had been so dry that the tips of grasses in the vacant lots and the leaves hanging down over the opening were yellowing.

Once they passed out of the sunshine, the air was cold, like it wasn't almost a hundred degrees that day. Ivy looked back toward the opening, at the summer day framed there, and the houses of Milltown beyond.

"You scared about going to the middle school this fall?" Greg said, and Ivy was grateful for the distraction. She shrugged and then realized that in the dark he couldn't tell she'd done so. "No," she lied.

"My sister Amy's going into seventh grade. You know her?"

Ivy thought: pictured a dark-haired girl in too-tight jeans, smoking. "I think so."

"I'll tell Amy to look out for you. She'll do what I tell her. Now in a minute we'll start to see the light at the other end. See, I bet Holly ran out the other side. She's probably sitting at your house right now, laughing at you."

"No," said Ivy, and here was where the ground turned suddenly downward, just like last time, leading them deeper into the earth, not out the other side. Here was where Holly had let go of her hand and grown quiet, then sidled up to her and shrieked right in her ear, panicking Ivy, and then there was something with them in the dark.

I dare you. That was what Holly had said, to

get her to go into the tunnel. *I dare you to go in there and call for Ash-Mouth. She lives in places like that, down in the dark, Nana said so.*

"That's weird," Greg said, "it doesn't go downhill here." But it did.

Ivy wanted to say *I told you so*, but that sounded bratty, people were always telling her she sounded bratty when she was only pointing out what she knew to be true.

As they descended the air was damp, not like above, and the sound of their breathing was matched by the drip of water on stone. Ivy put one hand out to feel her way through the blackness by touching the concrete wall, and snatched it back as her fingertips skidded across something slimy. Greg's voice came back, thin and insubstantial, as if he were disappearing just like Holly. "We'll see the other end. Just a few seconds now."

"Wait up," she said. She heard a noise and then Greg held a lighter above his head. He was a few feet in front of her, and in the flickering light he looked like a figure out of a horror movie, all eyes and cheekbones and teeth, and his face empty of color.

"Don't!" she cried, and ran to him, smacking his arm. Whatever had been in the dark with her and Holly before could probably find them with or without a light, but there was no need to expose themselves. The lighter clattered away and with the noise she realized the path beneath them was no longer dirt, but made of stone.

"Goddammit!" Greg said. "Now what are we gonna do?"

"I thought you knew your way."

"We should go back how we came," Greg said. "There must be a fork in the tunnel. I never heard of that before, but that must be it."

"Well," said Ivy, "you said you'd been down here a million times. Can't something change on the million-and-first visit?"

"That's the stupidest thing I ever heard. Like all the sudden the road starts going in a direction it never went before."

"Why not?" Ivy said. "Change is constant." That's what her father had said to her while she sat and watched him packing, putting shirts and socks and the ties she and Holly had given him over a lifetime of Christmases into a big hard-shelled suitcase. She had wished that he would cry or show some sort of emotion, but his eyes just stayed red and he said lots of things about how sometimes people needed to be apart from one another. And he said, *Don't think of it as something ending, Ivy; it's just change. Things change. One thing you can be sure of in life, change is constant. But it's nothing to be afraid of.*

He had been wrong, of course. Everything that mattered had changed.

"Roads don't change on their own," Greg said. "Not roads, or drainage pipes. Not solid things, just out of nowhere. We have to go back."

But they found they were turned around, and then they were arguing about which way would take them out and which would lead them deeper in, and Greg said, "Dammit, what did you make me drop my lighter for?" Ivy felt like she'd been spinning round and round in her father's office chair. She remembered reading somewhere about avalanches, how people died trying to dig their way out because they couldn't tell which way was up and only worked themselves deeper into the snow. She opened her mouth to warn Greg about that, and when she did the dark rushed in.

*

"Let's go in the living room," Nana said. "The news is fixing to come on. There's none of them left I know anymore," like the network anchormen were her neighbors. "You can stay for dinner if you like but I don't each much. I just heat up a can of soup."

"A can of soup is fine for me, Nana."

"Well, I only eat half the can at a time. I don't know if half a can is enough for you."

"I'm not really that hungry. I'm sure it will be all right."

The living room was as dismal as the kitchen had been, dark and chilly and, like the hallway, smelling faintly of something unpleasant that she couldn't identify. When had Nana's house become so inhospitable? It felt like the home of someone who could no longer manage to look after it, and maybe the coffee *had* been days old. Maybe Nana wasn't managing to clean or bathe or look after herself. Maybe Ivy's mother was right.

"Listen," she said. "Nana, listen to me. You've got to help me out here. Mama's talking like you need to go to a home and I've got to tell her something to reassure her. You have to stop calling her up and scaring her like you do."

Nana, sitting in a big armchair that made her look small and helpless, was blinking very rapidly. "Well," she said, and put down the cup of coffee she had brought in with her. "Well," she said again. "Well. I don't know how to answer that. Some of my group is coming over tonight. They don't treat me like a crazy person. They treat me the way family is supposed to. Maybe you ought not to stay here with them coming over."

Ivy kept her face expressionless when Nana talked about her group. The past few years she had attracted a flaky little assembly of lost souls, spiritual drifters who gathered round her after exhausting the extreme outposts of mainstream religions and the obscure secrets of the occult: they came trailing the detritus of Charismatic Christianity and Jewish mysticism, abandoning Sufi dervishes and flying yogis, pagan priestesses and Gnostic apologists. There was something pitiful in their easy acquiescence to belief—about which they were not choosy; any belief at all, it seemed, would do, and when one was used up they simply transferred their fervor to another. Faith was not a problem for them. Finding a suitable focus for it was the challenge, and in Nana they seemed to have done so at last. Ivy had seen them in a photograph Nana showed her once, and she would not have believed it if it had been described to her; an odder assortment of people she had never seen gathered together. They were clustered in front of the blooming dogwood in Nana's backyard: a small shrunken orange-haired woman with a hump on her back, twin albino boys, a small neat gentleman in a turban, a twenty-ish young man improbably clad in a vintage suit several generations older than he was.

Ivy took a deep breath. "Nana, I'm a scientist. I believe in things I can measure and observe, or at least extrapolate from my observations." She saw Nana blink at the word extrapolate and barreled on. "What I'm telling you is that I don't believe in any of these things. I don't believe in Ash-Mouth. It's just a story you made up when we were little. I don't know what happened to Holly, I can't even imagine, but I know Mama got it in her head that you had something to do with it and that's just crazy. I'm trying to help you out here. I'm on your side."

"You leave your mother to me," Nana said. "I can handle her just fine."

Ivy didn't know what she was going to say next until it was out of her mouth. "Nana," she said, "what really happened to my grandfather?"

*

"I loved him more than I have ever loved anyone, except for you girls, of course," Ivy's mother said. Ivy was sixteen and they were driving home from Boston, where she had been offered a full tuition scholarship to the aeronautics program at MIT. They were on the flat and uneventful stretch of highway between Charlotte and Greenville, and had been on the road for too many hours. "When he walked out the door like he did my heart broke, even though I was already grown up and living away from home by then."

Over the years, as Ivy's father had retreated from their lives (making a new life with a woman named Regina, whom Ivy loyally despised), her mother had increasingly turned to her as a confidante. It was a forced and uncomfortable intimacy, one-sided and painful.

"I hated her for a long time after that," Ivy's mother went on. "I wished she had died instead, and left him behind."

Ivy watched the billboard and exit signs slipping past, counted license plates from faraway states, prepared to suggest that they stop at a Waffle House where perhaps over runny eggs and lukewarm hash browns her mother's emotional revelations would be inhibited.

"She never even acted like she cared he was gone. What did she ever tell you about all that?"

Ivy was startled, like she'd been caught daydreaming in class. "What?"

"Ivy, you heard me."

"That he burned up." The words were out before she could stop them. She hoped that somehow her mother would mishear.

"*He burned up?*"

"Well . . ."

"That he *burned up*? My God, just when I think she can't surprise me anymore she goes and does it again."

The Moon Will Look Strange

"Don't tell her I said so," Ivy pleaded, but her mother was too angry to listen.

"She might as well have killed him." Her mother was rummaging in her purse for cigarettes and weaving a little as she did so. "She destroyed him before he left. I'm surprised he was able to get away. You're old enough to hear this now," but Ivy did not think she was, did not think she would ever be old enough to hear these sorrows and hatreds churned up like this. "She has no capacity for empathy. She's the most self-centered person I've ever met in my life." She retrieved her cigarettes and righted the car. "I won't let her rot away and die, because she's my mother, but that's just duty. And God, she's so overbearing. Do you know she insisted on naming you two?" She glared at Ivy, as though suddenly blaming her. "Honestly, Holly and Ivy. Such a ridiculous name for a set of sisters. Would it have been better or worse if you'd been twins? I don't know why I let her do it. She said you needed special names. So manipulative. Just like the old witch she wants everyone to believe she is."

Ivy thought about her friend Karen's mother, who was very sweet unless she was drunk. Sometimes, she thought, it would be easier to have a drunk for a mother, because then at least you could draw a definite line between the two states.

"You could always call me by my middle name," she suggested.

"Don't be ridiculous," her mother said, and they made the rest of the trip home in silence. That night Ivy heard her, for the first time in ages, moving about in Holly's room. For a few years after Holly's disappearance she spent a lot of time in there; sometimes she slept in Holly's bed. Ivy wondered how her mother would manage being all alone in the house once she moved a thousand miles away. The following day she announced that she really hadn't liked the campus at MIT, and even accounting for the tuition scholarship, she'd save money by living at home and commuting someplace local. Her mother agreed distantly, like Ivy was a long way off on the telephone, in a country far away.

*

Nana said, "I told you what happened to him. He just went away."

"You said he burned up."

"What?"

"When we were little. You said he had burned up. You showed us a picture."

"Of him burning?"

Ivy bit back an exasperated noise. "Not him. Someone else."

"Now, why would I do something like that? I always did say he smoked too much. I don't know. Maybe he did leave, or maybe he did burn up. I can't remember anymore."

Someone knocked at the front door. "That'll be Xerxes from my group, he's always early," Nana said. "Come in, Xerxes!"

"You shouldn't leave your front door unlocked like that."

Nana said, "It's not what's outside that I'm worried about."

The Moon Will Look Strange

*

That day in the culvert, when the neighbors had heard her screaming, this time louder and longer than the first so they realized it wasn't just kids playing games any longer, they thought at first that she had been attacked, because sometimes people did things like that, snatched little children and dragged them into places like the culvert and hurt them in the dark. When she was able to stop screaming she didn't mention Greg, because any way she tried to tell the story it came out wrong, and she was afraid he'd be blamed for whatever they imagined had happened to her—and to Holly—on that day.

Because they wouldn't have believed anything she told them; when people came into the tunnel to find her there, they didn't get lost. They didn't find it winding and twisting, making forks where it ought not to be, leading them into the center of the earth. Things just didn't change like that. Greg was right.

Some men from the sheriff's department, and her parents, had questioned her over and over again, and it always ended with her breaking down in tears; one of the deputies suggested that Holly had, in fact, run away, because there were no signs of what they called "foul play." Ivy saw the deputies exchanging looks with one another when her mother started shouting at them, asking what kind of policeman thought a twelve-year-old girl just up and ran off like that? Ivy knew that sometimes they did; she had seen television shows where troubled young kids ran away to big cities and got taken in by people who turned them into drug addicts and worse, but she wanted to tell the deputies that Holly wasn't like that, she was just a normal kid who didn't have any reason to run off.

Ivy told herself it had happened just like everyone said; her imagination had gotten the better of her, and if she thought about it too much she'd end up like her Nana, locked up somewhere with electricity shot into her brain. She would not tell anyone about the nightmares that did not dissipate at dawn but followed her throughout the day; that sometimes she had to shut her eyes to keep from seeing things lurking at the edge of her vision. It was a small price to pay for having escaped the madness that took Nana when she was young. Ivy threw herself into her schoolwork, and found that facts and figures anchored her to an earth that threatened to unbind her from its laws and logics.

She went to Greg's house once, partway through the school year. She had heard a rumor from a kid at school that he'd run off, too, but nobody had ever connected his disappearance with Holly's that day; maybe his parents had never even reported him missing, and someone else said no, he'd gone to live with his grandparents in Calhoun Falls. Ivy rang the doorbell and Greg's mother answered, still wearing a bathrobe and slippers even though it was four o'clock in the afternoon. She looked like an old woman, and reeked of alcohol. Ivy had no idea why she had gone there; she had not prepared herself for what she would do or say (she did not even know what to say to her own mother), and so she whispered, "I'm sorry, I have the wrong house," and ran away and told herself she would not think of it again.

*

"Come in, Xerxes!" Nana said again.

But there was no response, and no further knocking. Ivy went to the door herself. The front porch was empty, just dead leaves skittering across it in a gust of wind.

Nana seemed agitated when Ivy returned to the living room. She suggested dinner, and asked Ivy to go to the kitchen with her to heat the soup.

They ate in the living room, bowls on their laps, the television still flickering in the corner with the volume low. Nana was talking too much, about her group, about the past. "That summer," she said. "I was so sick. I don't even think I knew what had happened to Holly until I got better in the fall."

"What was wrong with you? Mama wouldn't tell us what you had."

Nana shook her head. "They didn't know. The doctors found all kinds of things wrong with me, just like I told them, but they couldn't figure out what was causing any of it. And then I got better."

"Holly was looking for Ash-Mouth," Ivy said. "She said we could find her and make sure she didn't try to take you away with her. I don't even think she believed that. I sure did. I was scared to death that day. But Nana, Ash-Mouth was just a story. You know that. I bet a house this old makes a lot of settling noises at night. That's what you're hearing."

Nana said, "Remember when I told you when you were older, I'd explain what was secret about the place where light met dark?"

"I think so."

"Here it is," Nana said. "Angels live in the light and demons in the dark. But what about the in-between, the places that are neither, or the space between the end of the light and the beginning of the dark?"

In the long silence that followed Ivy thought she heard, ever so faintly, the sound of someone whispering: then she realized it was only voices from the television.

Nana said, "The world's full of places like that. You can't hide from them forever. Even I can't. You should go now. You can't do anything for me. My group will be here soon and they'll sit with me and I promise I won't try to talk to your mother about it anymore."

*

Nana died the following year—presumably in peace, though Ivy could not shake the image of Ash-Mouth leaning over her frightened grandmother to suck the breath from her lungs, like the old wives' tales about cats and babies. She had not seen her Nana again since the night she'd tried to persuade her that Ash-Mouth did not exist, but Nana had stopped calling her mother and frightening her, and that was the important thing. Nana's "group" came for her funeral but kept to themselves; it had been Xerxes, the young man in the old suit, who found her.

The Moon Will Look Strange

Nana's funeral fell on a flawless spring day, with a sky so blue it broke Ivy's heart. Afterwards they all retired to Nana's house, her group included, where they ate and reminisced and Ivy and her mother began making plans to meet back in a few weeks to sort through Nana's things. Everyone remarked on how sunny and light the house seemed, and the funeral had been as nice as one as anybody could remember. Ivy left them to wander from room to room, but nowhere in evidence was the odor that had suffused Nana's house the previous year; it had come to her that night only as she was leaving, rising up like nausea, the source of the smell that she had not been able, until that moment, to name: it was the redolence of cold damp ashes.

Lynda E. Rucker

These Foolish Things

The party had begun to fill up with people and the beat of something Leon called post-dubstep that gave him a headache. He saw her across the room, and he pushed his way toward her and she turned and his drink hit the floor. The can rolled away spewing what was left of its insides but nobody really noticed and Leon's floor was kind of sticky anyway, like the floor of a club, because Leon was always throwing these parties, and he was always turning up at them. He didn't know why.

From across the room, he'd thought she had beautiful hair, that was all, glossy and black, just the way he liked it. He had not imagined that she would look exactly like Carla. The high forehead, the nose that was almost but not really too big, the wide violet eyes. Always her eyes. For a split second he wondered if she'd concealed the existence of a twin sister like she concealed so much about herself.

He couldn't stop himself from going up to her. He expected her to greet him like Carla would, with affection, but instead she smiled at him bemusedly, a pretty girl's tired smile poised somewhere in between do-I-know-you and fuck off. "Hey," he said, and she smiled at him again, a different smile this time—Carla's smile. He had felt—he could not say what he had felt, initially, but it had been something good; something hopeful had swelled within him but when he saw that smile it all evaporated. Like she was the thing that had taken Carla and turned her into someone he didn't know any longer, or maybe someone he'd never known.

A white and stark and blinding rage seized him. She flinched like she saw it too. He couldn't stop himself. "Carla, what are you doing here? Why are you doing this? Let's get out of here."

She was looking around as if for someone to save her from him (probably looking for that one guy, that bastard she'd slept with). "I'm sorry," she said, still casting her glance all around the room. "I'm sorry, you must have me confused with someone else. My name is Annie."

As if on cue, a burly guy with a big bushy beard was waving his arms at her from the corner where people were setting up instruments and plugging cords into amps and she said, "I have to do a sound check" and flashed another smile at him. Like that would make it okay.

She was laughing at him. They always did—the Carlas, the Annies, whatever they were called.

Someone cut the music for the sound check. If he were going to act, it needed to be fast. He lunged at her.

He saw her expression—fear, shock. Bushy Beard, surprisingly spry, was across the room in a flash, pulling her to imagined safety.

He said to no one in particular, least of all Bushy Beard, "That's my wife, dammit."

And behind him people were saying things like, "Dude," and Leon was beside him going, "What's the problem, bro?" Leon reeking of grass with his pupils so dilated you could fall into their blackness. "Maybe you better take a walk or something."

"I was invited here so you could all make fun of me, wasn't I? You all wanted me to see *her* and suffer."

Titters and whispers behind him, a girl with a dumb voice going, "Is he all right?" Did he look all right to her? All right, then.

Leon and another guy with wiry tattooed forearms—that was all he could really see, ink-splashed arms gripping his shoulders—were firmly guiding him out the door. Annie, or Carla, was safe on the other side of the room with a couple more guys around her. (How many of them was she fucking, anyway?)

Outside, the cool night air brought clarity. He started walking. He knew he'd see her again soon enough. At the end of the street of row houses he turned up toward the traffic and the noise.

She startled him, stepping from an alleyway into his path. The light of the blinking sign from the all-night diner down the street flashed on her face, turning it gruesome shades of red and green.

He said, "How could you do that to me?"

She laughed at him. "I'm not Carla," she said. "I'm not your Carla. I'm Jennifer."

He grabbed her arm, hard, and she didn't try to pull away.

She said, "You know I always liked it a little rough like that."

He twisted her wrist. He wanted to break it, he wanted her all broken, but she just laughed again.

"What are you looking for?" she said.

He was so angry he couldn't believe tears were stinging his eyes. "It's you," he said, "it's really you."

She said, "It's always me. It's never me. You get it wrong every time."

"Don't ever leave me," he said.

He had dropped any pretense now that he could hurt her. His arms hung limp at his sides.

"Why did you do it?" he said.

"Do what?"

"Everything."

She leaned toward him, her lips parting, and he thought she was going to kiss him, but she laughed.

She said, "I wanted more. I wanted the whole world. Your world was so small."

He said, "Don't. Don't you make me."

But she always did.

His fingers pressed into her throat but she was insubstantial as ghosts always are. She turned into rose petals; she turned into rain. She wasn't real and neither was he.

The last thing he saw before the world winked them both back out of existence was her beautiful face, her magical sorrowful violet eyes. The last thought he had was *who will you be next time? Gabrielle? Donna? Suji? Kris?*

The alleyway was so cold. The wind scraped old newspaper down the sidewalk; the moon rose full and high in the sky; the ghosts of lovers lost flickered like beacons in the night, and died again and again.

Lynda E. Rucker

Beneath the Drops

I usually tell this story in bars. I wait until it gets late and business has slowed down and it's just the bartender and me and two or three regulars dozing over their whiskey shots and warm beer. I'll tell it to you, though. I'm a good storyteller. Yes, it's very hot here. It's a dry heat, though. I chase after dry seasons like other people chase after money or fame or happiness. I like to stay on the move. I don't like damp climates, and I hate the rain.

*

Rain pelted the car the day we arrived in Oregon. Rain ran dirty in the ditches alongside the road and hampered our vision on that winding drive through the Cascades. All the while Gwen kept talking about Douglas firs and salmon and a mild climate, one that didn't make you wish you could crawl clean out of your skin six or eight months out of the year. "Look, Evan," she said to me over and over, pointing. I kept my eyes on the road and thought about home.

Gwen said she'd always wanted to go back to the Northwest, ever since her family moved away from there when she was little. She'd been born in the college town where I was accepted for grad school. We rented a house close to downtown and the university, the kind of area populated by students and junkies and worried-looking single moms still in their teens. She made friends right away at the little natural-foods grocery where she found work as a clerk. They sold organic everything and Sai Baba incense sticks and Rice Dream non-dairy bars. Her new friends had names like Pema and Rainbow, and they wore their hair in white-girl dreadlocks and carried battered copies of *The Monkey Wrench Gang* in their backpacks. They dropped in sometimes with their boyfriends. Greg and Riley were fey, stringy-haired guys with thin fingers that rolled endless nervous joints on our coffee table. They looked away from my collection of Italian horror videos, Bava and Fulci and Argento, like the sight might injure them. We skirted my taste in films and talked about other things.

By Christmas I was ready to go back home to Houston. I could already see I wasn't cut out for a career in academia. Not unless I wanted to drain every bit of life out of literature, suck out the marrow and grind down the bones for good measure. Gwen said I was lurking around the house too much, watching videos, hunched over the computer. I used to write articles for obscure zines about films only a few people had ever heard of. Gwen knew how I was; she'd lived with me long enough, and she had never complained about it in the past.

It didn't help that the rain shrouded the streets in a perpetual gloom that long winter, and mold thrived around the apartment so abundantly you'd have thought we cultivated it. From dotting the ceiling over the shower it spread like some damnable stain around the windowsill, and finally claimed clothes and books and papers stashed in boxes too long. I swore every time I found further evidence of its incursion, and bought bottles of cleaner that were supposed to control mildew but didn't.

Gwen just laughed at me when I told her about the patterns in the raindrops. "Listen," I said, but she didn't know how. When we went out at night, walking to the brewpub, inhuman shapes stalked us through the heavy air. Sometimes they came close enough for me to see that they were human after all. Other times they slipped away before we got a look at them.

"Cabin fever," Gwen said. "You should come out with us Friday. You'd like the music Riley's friend plays." Or she'd tell me, "Everyone wanted to know where you were the other night." But I felt ill at ease with her friends. We were an awkward mix; they were part of a different sort of life Gwen was fast acquiring for herself.

She liked the rain, and raised the windows in the early evenings so she could sit beside them with a cup of herbal tea. Said it soothed her, cleared her head after a bad day at the store. Working in her sketch book, or just staring out the window, she'd worry at her hair, which was in that awkward growing-out stage, orange on the tips from an old dye job. Sometimes she'd tap a charcoal pencil against her upper lip until she wore a little Fuhrer-like mustache right under her nose. As soon as she stirred, got up to pee or make a phone call or raid the refrigerator, I shut the window. I imagined the gloom outside dragging depressing entrails through our living room and bedroom and the little nook off the kitchen where we drank coffee together in the morning. When Gwen returned to her seat she would direct a heavy, obvious sigh at the closed window, but she never said anything about it.

*

Pema was the first person to mention Gwen's paintings to me. We were sitting on the sagging Goodwill-issue couch in the living room while Gwen was in back, changing to go out. "Have you seen what's she's been working on lately?" Pema asked me. She wore a permanent look of calm amazement, so I was never sure how excited she was about any given thing. I think almost everything impressed her.

I mumbled something. I was embarrassed to admit I didn't even know where her studio was. Some customer at the grocery had offered her the space cheap or maybe even free. Some guy I'd never met. Gwen had always been fiercely private. Back home she'd had friends she saw regularly that she never introduced me to. I'd liked that about her. She had her own life and I had mine. But this felt like a deliberate shutting-out.

"They're really trippy," Pema said. "You should check them out when you get a chance. She's got a lot of talent."

I couldn't argue with that, but Pema annoyed me, with her outmoded slang and earnest way of speaking. Outside the rain rattled its fingers down the window pane, and clouds muffled the sounds.

"Did you hear that?" I said, and Pema asked

what, and I didn't know how to describe it. I'd never gone so long without seeing the sun. I dreamed of it sometimes, and woke up with blinding headaches after nights spent wandering on sweltering treeless landscapes.

"Is your name really Pema?" I asked her. "I've never known anyone named that before."

"It's my Buddhist name." She didn't volunteer another. I wanted to ask, but knew better. It was the key. Behind the latter day hippie costume lay a middle class girl still trying to piss off her parents.

"Are you?"

"Am I what?"

"Buddhist."

"Oh. Yeah." She picked at cotton threads on her blouse. "It's what it's all about, man. Non-attachment. And non-violence." She flapped her hand toward a stack of my videos. "Why would you want to watch anything like that? Do you like it?"

"That stuff? It's like Grand Guignol." I could tell she didn't know what I was talking about, and a little burst of superiority egged me on. "Those videos don't have anything to do with what you're talking about." But Gwen interrupted us then, had come in the room and was pulling on her mittens.

"Sure you don't want to come?" Gwen called over her shoulder as they stepped outside. The door swung shut before I could answer them. I couldn't remember where they were going, only that it hadn't sounded like something I would enjoy.

I got a cold pint of Rainier out of the fridge and settled in on the couch for a zombie double feature. Twenty minutes into it, I'd paused the tape three times, distracted by a wet, squelching noise. Maybe a leak dripping onto an already-saturated carpet, although that would have to be one hell of a drip to hear it above the movie. Then I thought it might be the video itself, because every time I stopped it, the noise stopped too. But it wasn't the kind of sound a faulty tape would make.

It was a pattern, though, that something might follow if it was trying very hard not to be heard. Waiting till the screaming on the video was loud enough that a fair amount of noise would go undetected. Spooked, I took the coward's way out—I turned up the volume so loud I couldn't even hear anything over the quieter parts.

Before starting the second movie I got up for another beer. Then a detour up the hall to the bathroom, and that was when I realized the carpet was soaked. Not a leak, though. These were concentrated patches of damp, like something with wet feet had been wandering up and down the hall.

I stood there a moment or two in the near-dark, gazing at mine and Gwen's bedroom, then stepped forward and switched on the light. It flooded an empty room. I felt like my grandmother, checking the closet, peeking under the bed, tugging at the window locks to make certain that they were secure. The damp patches spotted the carpet in there, too.

When I got back from the bathroom, I put the unopened beer back in the fridge and turned on the rest of the lights in the house. I played with the remote until I came to one of the most banal things I could find—one of those "reality" shows on MTV. Two housemates were fighting. One of them called the other a bitch.

I went back in the kitchen and rummaged under the counter until I found the closest thing to strong drink we had, some cheap sherry we sometimes used for cooking. It tasted like hell. I got one glass down without choking on it. The rain outside gave me a forlorn, marooned feeling. When I looked out, I couldn't see any of the other houses.

Oregon rain is rarely heavy, or accompanied by storms. An incessant mist, a steady drizzle, thickens the air. You can't go anyplace without an umbrella because you never know when it might start up again. West of us, rivers were rising, towns flooding. I might have been underwater at that moment, for all I could see beyond the window.

Some people blamed the timber industry and its clear-cutting, and the folks who built their homes on cliff edges without regard for environmental degradation. Gwen said the flooding was almost Biblical, like some ancient god had been awakened and angered. This was no seasonal happening, like tornadoes in the Midwest or fire and mudslides in California. This was something new for people. We'd seen one man on the news, shaking his head and looking like he'd been clobbered with something. "They told us this was a hundred-year flood plain," he said. His face was bleak. "I didn't know we had anything to worry about."

I didn't know we had anything to worry about. But I guess everyone thinks that, right up until the moment they lose everything.

The front door slammed. "Shit!" Gwen said. "What's going on in here?" She had the remote in her hand when I went back in the living room, and she'd muted the volume. "You want all of the neighbors to get their *Real World* fix, too?"

"How did you find the house through all that?" I said to her back as she retreated up the hall, and then was glad that she didn't seem like she'd heard me. "I think we've got a leak or something," I called more confidently. She still didn't say anything. Her coat, draped across the back of the couch, smelled of pot and patchouli.

"Did you have fun?" I followed her, and called through the bathroom door over the sound of running water.

She shouted something back. I couldn't hear her. She opened the door, just enough to show me that she was brushing her teeth, then slammed it again.

"I'll tell you about it later," she said when she left the bathroom, "I'm tired now," and the last thing she did before crawling into bed and pulling the covers up tight was open both windows so the sound and scent of rain filled the room.

*

Maybe it was around that time when I started thinking of her as two different people, the "old Gwen" and "new Gwen". It's an ugly, corrosive thing couples do, holding one another responsible for not remaining the same person year after year. I did it anyway. The first night she didn't come home I wasn't really surprised. I was less concerned about ferreting out the truth of her whereabouts, whether she'd spent the night with a lover or alone at her studio, than I was with the fact of her absence, the suspicion that it was the start of a more permanent situation.

So I tried to remind her of things that would make her laugh, silly private jokes between the two of us. The time a road trip to visit some friends in Georgia took us through a town called Dacula where, giddy with too much driving, we were suddenly struck with the necessity to read every sign we passed in a bad Transylvanian accent. "Dacula Auto Parts, bleh, <u>bleh</u>." The family we'd inadvertently terrorized at the beach the year before, when the hotel gave us the key to an occupied room—I'll never forget the look on the guy's face as he grabbed, I swear to God, a *baseball bat* leaning up against the wall, in arm's reach of the bed. It was like he'd been waiting all his life for one of those "home invasion robberies" he'd heard about on the news. Gwen and I fled, overcome with hysterical adrenaline giggles, and it was half an hour before we could compose ourselves enough to return to the front desk. So many little cues that become a kind of shorthand between two people who are close to one another, things you could never explain to anyone else because they just aren't amusing in the retelling. It seems like those things should bind you, but they don't. They stopped being funny to Gwen. She would just smile at me like she was being polite and talk about something else.

When I knew she wasn't listening at all, I tried asking about her work. She replied in monosyllables. "Can I see some of it, when you're done?" I asked, and tried to pretend her acquiescence had not been grudging.

The Moon Will Look Strange

At night, when she was out, I took walks round our neighborhood, where water dripped from branches above onto my hatless head and down the collar of my coat. Along the riverbanks trees gave up the ghost, toppling over, their roots unable to find purchase in the saturated soil. A coastal town north of us vanished under twenty feet of water.

While I listened to the rain and Gwen went out with the girls or worked at her studio, Greg and Riley rapped with me about whatever captured their short attention spans. Earth First and the magazines I wrote for, the quality of Oregon versus California weed and good swimming holes for summer trespassing, the families that didn't understand them and the tiny desert towns in the eastern part of the state they both came from and the rain. Always the rain. "A deluge," Riley pronounced. Greg added, "Never seen it like this before." But their observations were hazy, drug-enhanced, in love with the act of talking itself as much as anything. And then sometime after Christmas they stopped coming around. I was surprised to find that I missed them. For all that we had nothing in common, they'd been human contact, something I had precious little of. I'd quit going to classes at all at that point and when my student loan check ran out I was going to have to make a move pretty fast. I'd already decided to leave. All I had to do was persuade Gwen to go with me.

On one of the last nights that Greg and Riley did drop in, we'd lounged around the living room smoking cigarettes and arguing about something I don't remember, something that had mattered very much to them and not even a little to me. I can't remember why I argued with them—and it wouldn't help even if I could remember what it was about. Something about those two just made me want to challenge them. They'd left late, and I sat up to drink one last beer. I heard them back again, at the front door.

"Your van giving you problems—" I said as I swung the door open; Riley had mentioned trouble with the starter. But there was nothing outside but the grey steady rain.

"Ha, funny, guys," I said, just in case, even though I knew they were both gone.

And took a few steps forward. Only a few. It was no more than four or five, off the front concrete stoop and into the yard. The mist swirled and closed round me. An engine chugged and failed to catch somewhere ahead and to the right.

"Riley?" I said, and went toward it. It occurred to me then that I couldn't see the van, not even the shape of it, through the mist and rain. I whirled round; the house had vanished. The feeling I'd had previously, of being marooned as I looked out from the window, rushed back. If I had turned at that moment, gone back in a straight line, I might have come to the house again. I might have just taken those few paces right back in the direction I'd come and found myself where I started. But I might not have, and I'll never know, because what I actually did was panic, and stumbled forward, toward where I thought the van should be. "You guys can come on in and call somebody if you need to," I said wildly, blindly, because I knew Riley and Greg were long gone and I was talking to something else making the sound, but hoping against hope they'd step out of the gloom and I wouldn't be alone. I continued forward. At any moment, whatever direction I traveled in, I must hit a street—we lived in a dense residential area of pre-war houses and cheap sixties-boom apartment buildings. There were other people all about me, and yet they seemed to have vanished.

When I thought of the road I looked down, but I couldn't see the ground at all. I could barely see my feet. Only the thick white mist curling round my ankles, my calves. I cried out and stumbled backwards. I thought of the shapes, the squelching noises, the things that moved ponderously in the night and the way that Gwen let the rain in whenever she could. I ran, flailing at the air around me as if warding off attackers. Beneath my feet a ground slick and muddy sucked at my shoes. I imagined the deluge coming at any moment, the floods that had taken other towns around us arriving here all at once, twenty feet of water smashing down upon me and how strange it would feel to find myself adrift and drowning in my own neighborhood.

Slam! Right into the stop sign on the corner. I reeled backward, fell on my ass. I really did see stars. Touched my face and was relieved to feel nothing more than a swelling, bloody lip. I could look down and see blood diluted pink dripping onto my shirtfront. I had run across four lots of houses to reach this corner and seen and heard nothing but the rain. Holding my shirt to my lip, I got up and followed the sidewalk back home.

I didn't look out the window anymore that night.

Lynda E. Rucker

*

Later on, Gwen asked me if I wanted to come to her studio and see what she'd been working on.

To say that I was caught off guard is an understatement. I'd fully expected her to keep putting me off indefinitely, the issue forever unresolved. The day she suggested it I thought of her as "old Gwen". I'd taken a job at the 7-11 down the street to make ends meet, and had a rare morning off with her. We'd made pancakes and coffee that was too strong, and we were watching the cartoon network on TV.

"Today?" I said stupidly, and Gwen said, "Now." Our pancakes weren't eaten yet, still nearly whole and drenched in syrup, but I was afraid to put her off even for half an hour, as though she might change her mind in that time.

Somehow I'd imagined we'd drive far out of town to get to the fabled studio, down some wooded dirt road into the middle of nowhere, as though crossing a threshold. Of course that wouldn't have been practical at all for her, and the studio was less than ten minutes from our house, right around the corner from the Safeway where we did most of our grocery shopping. I wanted to ask her why she'd never mentioned it before, and of course I didn't.

The studio was in back of an older house. "Garth's ex-wife was an artist," she said, inclining her head toward it, casual as though the three of us were all great friends. "He was going to tear down her studio when they split up, but then he said he figured why not let somebody who needs it use it for free?"

The Moon Will Look Strange

She looked back at me like she was testing my reaction. "I won't have it forever, though. He lives down in the Bay Area. He's going to put this on the market soon."

The studio proper was little more than a gardening shed, albeit with plenty of windows. You could see where there would be a lot of light, if there was any to be had in the winter gloom.

Gwen fumbled with keys. "Remember that one show I did before we left Houston?" she asked. "I've gone in a completely different direction now." The door swung open and an unwelcome but familiar smell greeted us. "These are pretty non-representational, so I don't know how much of it you'll get." I ignored the snide remark and identified the smell: damp. Mildew. And mold.

The interior was darker than I'd thought it would be. The sheer number of canvases, many of them only half-finished, surprised me. I opened my mouth to ask her where she'd gotten the money for all the supplies and immediately thought better of it.

At first neither one of us said anything, as I wandered from piece to piece, trying to take it in, trying hard to think of something to say about these abstract swirls of blue and green and black smeared before me. Sometimes the effect was mottled rather than swirled. "These are interesting textures," I said at last, and that was true, and better than the only other thing I could think to say about the piece I stood in front of. Mainly that it resembled nothing so much as the mildew blotches above the shower in our bathroom.

It began to rain steadily, streaking the windows. As I stood before another painting, looking from it to the window and muddy yard outside and back again, I saw the connection: this one, a swirl of blues and greys, imitated the streaks on the smudged windowpane.

"Rain," I said, and didn't know I'd spoken out loud until Gwen answered behind me.

"Yes, that's going to be the name of my new show. Garth knows a gallery owner who wants to do it, and I'm scheduled to hang it next month."

"Gwen," I said without turning around to look at her, "it's really damp in here. Are you sure it's okay to keep all your stuff in this? And what do you know about this Garth guy, anyway?"

I could tell as soon as it was out of my mouth that it was the wrong thing to say.

We drove home without talking. She didn't mention the paintings or upcoming show to me again.

*

What she said, days later when she finally really talked to me was, "It's not you. It's me."

She said all the things to me people say when they are breaking up with you but don't quite have the courage to do so. At this point it was a little bit like holding a funeral after the corpse had been rotting in the back room for weeks. She sat at the card table in the kitchen when she told me. We called it the kitchen table, like that made it fancier than it really was.

"You're goddamn right it's not me," I said. It felt good to get angry at her.

The Moon Will Look Strange

"Why are you so hostile?" Gwen asked. She never used to use words like that. Her hair had grown a few inches since we moved there, and she looked young and lost. I wanted to hit her. I'd never wanted to do anything like that before.

"I'm not hostile!" I shouted at her, and I hated the way she flinched. "It's this goddamn *place* and all your goddamn *friends*—"

Her face reddened. She hadn't been angry before, but she was now. "My goddamn friends are right about *you*," she shouted back.

After that there wasn't anything more to say. She started to cry, like a kid after a tantrum. I held her. Her skin felt damp and clammy. I smoothed down her hair and said soothing things and then I tried to kiss her.

"Stop it," she said, and pulled away from me. Dark patches like bruises had appeared where I'd touched her arms.

I wanted to talk to her more. I wanted to tell her about the shapes, the things moving about at night, the smells under dead wet leaves and soggy rocks and fetid soil.

"I'm sorry," she said, but she wasn't.

That night I dozed on the couch, watching infomercials for impossible pieces of exercise equipment and headline news that recycled itself every thirty minutes. She was awake in our bedroom. I heard her moving around in there, but I didn't go to her, and she didn't come out to me. The rain was louder than usual that night. Between the drops something mocked me.

We lived that way for a while after, Gwen and I, under a pained, unspoken truce. Eventually I moved back into the bedroom and she slept there beside me at night, cold and unresponsive. She looked thinner and paler as the winter wore on, shadows beneath her eyes. I noticed bruises at the edges of her clothes, along her collarbone, her forearms. Sometimes, when I brushed against her, her skin was moist, like a sponge that needed wringing out.

I talked to her sometimes like she was still the old Gwen. I talked about going home, about restaurants she'd liked and old friends and sandy beaches with water warm enough to swim in. If I didn't keep talking about home I would find myself telling her that I was working out the patterns in the rain, that the shapes had begun to turn toward me in the night, like they knew I knew. I need not have talked about anything. She wouldn't have noticed.

Her absences lengthened. She had a show coming up, after all. She'd neglected to tell me—when we were on better terms—where the gallery was, and it was too late for me to ask, just as concern about her health and physical well-being was off-limits to me now. Anything might be construed as prying, now that we were merely roommates biding time. She saw it like that, anyway. On nights when she was out with her friends and not at the studio I watched movies with the volume turned up loud so I could not hear the squelching sounds of things that moved about the house, searching for her.

*

The Moon Will Look Strange

I was home alone the last night, as usual, working on an overdue article. The hammering at the door sounded like what cops do when they mean business.

But it was only Pema on the other side of it. I was irritated as I swung it open, and even more so when I saw her standing there. She looked anxious and diminished.

"Have you seen Gwen much lately?" she asked.

I didn't let her in. Her interruption irritated me. "No," I said, closing the door partway. "We aren't exactly together any more, you know."

"I think you ought to check on her," she said.

"I don't think it's any of my business now."

"No one's seen her for three days."

I tried to think when I'd last seen her. The last weeks had been a blur, of her gone and then suddenly back again. I didn't know when she'd been home last.

"Call out the posse, then," and this time I did shut the door. And opened it again right away. I was never good at that kind of drama. Pema still stood there, patient, like she'd known exactly what I was going to do.

"So, what do you have in mind?"

"We could go to her studio and see how she is."

"I don't think you need me to do that. Actually, I think you're better off <u>not</u> bringing me along."

Pema just stood there. I didn't shut the door again.

"You're still closer to her," Pema said. "You should come. She might listen to you."

Closer to me indeed. If none of her friends knew how she felt about me any longer then she had been more successful than I'd imagined at compartmentalizing her life. It wouldn't do either of us any good for me to show up there in some final desperate act of—what? Reconciliation? Salvation? Maybe it was right though—maybe it would be the final break needed. I, at least, needed to see the breach between us widened beyond any hope of reconciliation.

Gwen had the car, so Pema and I took the bus down past the ugly stretch of warehouses and fast food places to the Safeway in the west part of town. I looked at her beside me and realized that she knew I wasn't going to be able to persuade Gwen of anything. Pema was afraid of something else. She didn't share it with me, though, on the ride out. An old woman in front of us who smelled bad and wore bright bright rouge and clumpy mascara chanted," You leave me *alone*, leave me *alone*" softly under her breath over and over, and the rain drizzled down the windows of the bus.

Pema trailed behind me as we walked away from the stop. Now that the moment had come I wanted to hasten it. I all but jogged down the side street where Gwen's studio was, slowing only when I started to become disoriented.

"What?" Pema said.

"You've been there more than I have," I said, losing patience with her now. "I thought it was right in this stretch here, but I don't see *Garth's* house."

"Who's that?" Pema said, and at the same time she veered off the sidewalk and cut across the gravel drive off a boarded-up old house that looked past due for its condemnation notice. In the backyard a forlorn shed on the verge of collapse sagged near the back fence. As I got closer my feet slipped in mud, and it clung to my shoes.

Pema, behind me, kept saying something, but I wasn't paying attention to her any longer. The door hung by one rusty hinge. I stood there for a moment, waiting for my eyes to adjust to the dinginess. I took a step forward, then another. The first thing that caught my eye was one of Gwen's mittens, discarded on the floor. It was soaking wet and looked like it had been there a long time.

The damp had spread everywhere. Great patches of it, and then smaller ones, like the traces of footprints from our house. Most of Gwen's canvasses were gone, a few forlorn stragglers leaning up against one wall, rain-spotted.

"Evan," Pema said, but the way she spoke my name I hardly recognized it.

She'd moved to the far corner, away from the door, and beside her was Gwen. Only not Gwen, a silhouette of Gwen on the wall, shadowed dark with damp and mold. Gwen's medium height, slim body, even the unruly tufts of her hair that had always maddened her by sticking up like little horns.

I couldn't see her face. I had no way of knowing how she felt about where she'd gone. Her arms were splayed out against the wall—she might have been lifting them in defense, supplication.

Or, she might have been welcoming something.

Pema's soft sobs broke the silence. They only made me angry. The damp there, it seeped into my flesh and my bones and my lungs and coiled in my soul. A dead wet cold, and patting gently on the roof above us, as always, the rain.

*

You can guess the rest. Not long after, I woke from a nightmare of drowning on air thick with rain. I'd dreamed I heard her voice beneath the drops. I didn't wait till dawn, not that it mattered in that unchanging gloom. I got in the car we'd shared and I drove and I didn't look back.

I heard about a place, in Chile, I think, supposed to be the driest place on earth. A giant desert. There are places there with names like the Salt Mountains and the Valley of the Moon. Used to be the bottom of an ocean, once upon a time. I might go there. I'd look for fossils of petrified seashells, and the blasted remains of those first jelly-like ocean creatures that squirmed onto land. But I guess that's all gone to dust now. I'd like it if that happened to me, if I got so dry I split apart and scattered across a thousand miles and you couldn't even find any pieces of me, even if you looked for another million years. There'd be nothing but the stars near enough to touch and the arid timbre of quiet, and not even that ocean coming back would matter to me anymore.

The Moon Will Look Strange

These Things We Have Always Known

Cold Rest is the name of this hard town scratched out on the side of a Georgia mountain ridge, so far to the north it's bleeding over into North Carolina, really, although it doesn't seem much to belong to either place. The people here have a certain way of talking, like you'll find in isolated regions, the kinds of places no one ever really leaves and that outsiders never move to, or even visit.

I have always known that there was something wrong in Cold Rest. People round here laugh when they say, something in the water, but it's true that the community my wife was raised in is not like other places. And there is a hardness about every single resident of Cold Rest—Sarah included—that is, in the end, like living alongside something rigid and alien. It hasn't been a perfect relationship; in twenty years we've had plenty of opportunity to hurt one another. I think Sarah still gets the occasional note or email from the man she thought about leaving me for (though she never would have) five years ago. You learn to overlook these things. Here in Cold Rest, things are different, as I have said.

That something was always waiting in Cold Rest we all knew. You often had the feeling that you were in a room with someone, even when alone, who was getting ready to speak, making barely audible noises prior to forming actual words. You felt it sometimes like a seismic rumble deep in the earth. When you dreamed it you never could remember the following day, just a kind of uneasiness like something had crawled into your brain in the night and left the faintest of markings behind, a gloss of breath where your own thoughts used to lie.

*

"That one's lovely, Neil." Until Sarah spoke I didn't know she'd been watching me. She came forward and touched the robin I'd been carving as gently as if it had been alive. Dusk had descended while I was out there in my little workshop at the back of the house. I had lost track of time.

Sarah frowned when she saw what else I was working on, an abstract sculpture about half her height, rusted wire twisted into irregular angles broken by slivers of mirror. Everywhere that the robin whittled out of oak was warm and comforting, this seemed designed to inflict a kind of wound upon the observer. I worked on the robin when I got blocked on the other piece.

"I wish you'd just stick to carving birds and dogs like you used to," she said. "You never made anything like this before."

I just shrugged.

"Dinner's ready. And Gary's here."

That surprised me. I hadn't heard my brother's truck—though it's true that I sometimes get so engrossed in my work that I am not really aware of anything outside it—and Gary hadn't dropped in to see us in a long time. He lived a couple of hours away, so it wasn't as though he'd just stop in casually.

I looked over the robin I'd been carving, ran one finger along its breast, felt something stirring. It seemed finished.

"What does he want?"

Sarah said, "I think he wants a job."

*

My brother's a writer—no, you probably haven't heard of him; when he tells people the names he writes under you can see them being sorry they've asked, anxious in case it turns out the names *ought* to ring a bell.

Gary prefers to think of himself as a regular guy. I know because he's told me so many times. He writes horror, thrillers, crime, whatever he can get paid for—Sarah says a romance novel here and there, though he's never admitted it to <u>me</u>—and that seems all right to him because it's regular-guy fiction.

We were sitting down to dinner, the four of us—our teenaged daughter Emma crept out of her room and joined us—and I said it outright. "I don't know, Gary. I mean, I'm sure I could get you on at the yard, but why in hell you want to go and do something like get a job? And why here?"

Gary looked at his food and mumbled. "Headaches. I've been getting these damn fierce headaches. I don't have any health plan and I'm scared to see a doctor. Something's really wrong, I could be paying them off for the rest of my life."

There was a silence round the table, except for

the sound of Emma's chewing with her mouth open.

Gary tried to laugh. "Thought I'd try to get me some of that sick leave you working folks are always talking about. Imagine getting paid to lie in bed all day and puke!"

I said, "It doesn't really work that way," but Sarah cut me off with a look.

"Besides," Gary went on, "the things that go on here sometimes with those carvings you do, I figure maybe I could use a jolt of that for my books."

Sarah said, "It doesn't happen the way you tell it to, Gary. Neil's carvings come to life under his hands sometimes, but it's not anything he can control. You can't use it for your own purposes."

When Sarah says *come to life* you understand that she is not speaking figuratively. I have told that you Cold Rest is not like other places.

"Well," Gary said, "I'd sure like a chance to try."

Sarah changed the subject. "How's Barbara?" she asked, referring to Gary's long-time, on-again off-again girlfriend.

"She got married last month."

Emma scraped her chair back and announced that she was going out. Her hair was black as pitch that night and falling across her face. The week before it was emergency-red. It was as though someone different sat down to dinner with us every few nights, although even without the outlandish hair I felt like I didn't know her any longer. She's grown so tall in the last couple of years, and her hands are long and delicate, pianist's hands, except she hasn't touched Sarah's grandmother's baby grand in the living room since she reached her teens. She has dark eyes and her mouth is sulky, at least around Sarah and me. Sarah said she was sure Emma and her boyfriend were having sex, but that she didn't know what to do about it. I said, I'm sure you'll handle it, because I didn't even want to think of it, and I didn't know why we had to *do* anything. That boyfriend of hers, Sam or Simon… What kind of a name is Simon anyway? I tried not to look at him when he came to visit. He had soft, puffy hands. I imagined saying something to him like, "You'd better not touch my daughter with those hands!", fully realizing how ridiculous that made me. I said to Sarah, "For God's sake, she's only sixteen years old," and she said, "But don't you remember sixteen? She seems like a baby to us but at sixteen you think you're all finished growing up."

But. Sixteen! She still looked like a child.

"I'll see what I can do for you," I said to Gary. "You can stay here if you need to. There's not much in town in the way of rentals."

"Why don't you take Gary out to your shop and show him what you've been working on?" Sarah suggested. "Maybe he'll like them better than I do."

Gary always feigned, or perhaps genuinely felt, a polite interest in even my most banal creations. We walked out there while Sarah was brewing coffee. Evenings in Cold Rest are beautiful. There's a special way the sun slips down the mountain and leaves everything glowing. Tonight we were just in time to see the sky deepen and blaze in all its twilight glory. I dragged a couple of the things I'd been working on out of my shop, because I'd noticed that when the light was right—at about that time of day—the metal

I was using glowed like it was plugged into an electrical outlet.

Gary didn't touch any of it like he usually does. He stood back a bit and pointed at one of them. "What's going on there?" he asked.

I had stretched and hammered torn strips of canvas across an irregularly-shaped cage I'd built, and along the sides threaded teeth from the skulls of dead animals I'd come across in the woods.

"I don't know," I said. "I just felt like it had to look that way."

Gary didn't say anything for a long time. Finally, "I don't like it."

That shocked me, and it hurt a little. Gary always liked what I did. He was younger than me, but I treated him more like an older brother, anxious for his approval. I'd never been real proud of my woodworking before, mediocre stuff I could've sold at inflated prices in some of the tourist towns to folks who didn't know any better. For the first time, making these sculptures that came to me in dreams, I felt like I was doing something that mattered.

"I think you ought to get rid of them and go back to making birds and baby rabbits, even if some of them do get away from you," he said, and then he was heading for his truck just like he hadn't said he was going to sit a while and have coffee with Sarah and me, and she came out the back door when she heard his engine and looked at me with a question in her eyes. Had we argued? I shook my head, to show her I didn't know.

*

The Moon Will Look Strange

The following evening, when I got out to the shop after work, I found the robin with its neck broken. I'd forgotten to set it outside before I closed up for the night, and it had flown repeatedly against the windows.

I cradled it in my palms and carried it in to show to Sarah and Emma. I felt so bad, like I'd taken it up in my own two hands and dashed it against the wall. Like I'd created something just so it could suffer and die. We buried it in the backyard because it didn't seem right to just throw it out, and Emma set a little ring of stones round its grave.

Sarah teaches English at the local junior high school in town. At night sometimes, to help me unwind, she reads me poems. I like the ones that rhyme. I know that's not very sophisticated of me, but there it is. My favorite poet is Robert Frost. Emma said, "Sean (or Stan, or Steve, or whatever his name is) is a poet and he said Robert Frost was supposed to have been a real dick." Sarah said, "Emma!" and Emma said, "What? I'm just saying," and I didn't say anything at all. Instead I repeated lines of poetry to myself. I like the one about miles to go before I sleep.

Sarah had Emma's boyfriend in her class a few years ago. She said he "had quite a way with words for such a young person." This made me feel like she was taking sides with Emma and that boy, against me. Sarah writes poetry, just for herself. Once in a while she'll read one to me. They don't rhyme, and I don't understand them, although I pretend like I do. I think this is one of the things she liked about the man she had the affair with. He was a poet of moderate renown—if you move in those circles, which I don't; I took Sarah's word for it—and she met him when she taught in a special program down south for gifted children a few summers ago. I remember how she was for a while afterwards. Not better, not worse, just a different Sarah; their intimacy drew out dormant parts I'd not known in her. She used words and turns of phrases she hadn't before. Her mind strayed to subjects I was unaccustomed to. They weren't his words, his subjects. They belonged to Sarah, but it was all hidden geography in the context of <u>our</u> relationship.

Maybe that was why she and Gary didn't like what I was working on. Maybe it was as simple as that, the unaccustomedness, the fact that they were used to seeing me work with wood and blade to make cozy scenes like fox families or spring fawns. I told myself that while she read to me that night by the fire, got lost in the words she was speaking till I fell asleep dreaming of the bird pitching itself against the glass, trying to get free, until it shattered the bones in its neck, and she had to wake me to send me to bed.

*

I knew that Emma was gone almost before she actually left. I thought afterwards about that word—*almost*—such a little word, six letters and the difference between what was and what might have been. I woke covered in a bad dream, and I felt something wrong in the night. Something gone out of the house. Later, when I talked to Sarah about it, she said I must have woken up earlier, unknowing, when

The Moon Will Look Strange

Emma closed the front door, or heard the engine of whatever car swept her into the night and away from us. I told her she must be right. But I knew what woke me was the simple fact of her absence, unnatural and complete. The house fairly vibrated with the lack of her. Had I known, in my dreams, that she was going? Had I let her go, to find out how far away she could get?

I was right all along not to trust that boy.

*

The week after Gary came to dinner—before Emma had left us—he accompanied me to the yard for the first time. I showed him round a little bit, and he went to talk to Human Resources, a phrase which has always had a little too literal a turn to it for my liking.

Gary talked a good game about honest manual labor but he's never been the type to break a sweat, and I knew he'd wind up taking a position in the office. I can't blame him for that. It gets unbearably hot in the yard in summer, and in the winter the ground freezes hard. I've seen folks felled by heat stroke and frostbite and worse things, because of what it is we're digging out of the ground there. And we sink mine shafts deep into the earth, even though it's getting harder to find people willing to go under the ground like that. Mostly just the old-timers'll take that kind of work.

Gary moved into our spare room, and he got up and went to work every day, and locked himself away when he came home, only venturing out for dinner. I figured he must be getting a lot of writing done. It got so we were seeing more of Emma than him, and that's saying something. I didn't pay him much attention, to be honest, because I'd been dreaming again about what I wanted to work on next, and the dreams were strange and left me with a taste in my mouth like cold metal. I didn't have clear pictures in my head of the devices I needed to build next, but the designs seemed etched into the movement of my hands.

And then Emma was gone, and the work was all that could soothe me, take my head somewhere it wasn't worried sick about what was happening to her. The police said they'd do all they could, and none of her friends knew a thing. Sean's—or Seth's—or Sam's mother visited Sarah one day; I couldn't bear to be around her, a wan, ineffectual woman. I headed out to the shop.

After a while Gary joined me. I was painting sheets of tin in coat after coat of black paint. I wanted to get a deeper black than I'd ever seen in nature. I asked Gary if he thought it was working. He didn't answer me.

"How are things going?" I said. "You seem pretty busy."

He shrugged and wouldn't look at me. "I've been writing," he said, "but when I get back and look at the pages, I don't remember putting down what I see there, and what I see scares me."

"What do they have you doing in the office there?" I was curious; there was no mixing between the blue- and white-collar folks at the yard.

"I print reports and collate them, and compare

long lists of figures with other long lists, but listen to this, after I get far enough down the lists they stop being numbers and they start being other kinds of marks, things I've never seen before. Also, I write letters for some of the executives. I wrote down the names of some of the places they were being sent to, places I never heard of, but when I looked them up later I could never find any of them." His face looked clammy and pale when he was telling me this.

"You made an appointment to see a doctor about those headaches yet? I know one in town'd see you."

He shook his head. "I don't think this has anything to do with those headaches."

"Still." I had a feeling Gary'd come to us because he was at the end of his rope, that it had been more than headaches and fear of skyrocketing medical bills that had driven him. I didn't know how to ask him if he had any money at all, but I didn't need to; knowing Gary, he'd have offered to pay us for room and board if he'd been able.

"Listen, Neil, I got to ask you something that sounds crazy. Do you ever think maybe you wind up in a place and everything in your life has been about moving you to that moment, preparing you for something momentous even? Like your life's work?"

"I hope you're not talking about Cold Rest. Anything moving you toward something here can't be good."

"Why'd you stay?"

"Why do people stay anywhere? My family's here."

"Why do *they* stay?"

They don't, I wanted to say, but I couldn't think that way. Emma would come back to us. It was simply not possible to acknowledge any other outcome. "It's different for folks born here."

Gary put his hand out to touch the piece I was working on. "Careful," I said, "wet paint," but wet paint or no, I didn't want anyone touching those structures but me.

"What are they?"

"Instruments," I said. "Instruments for the summoning of dead races."

"The hell's that supposed to mean? That sounds fucked up."

"It came to me. In a dream. I thought about trying to put on some kind of show, you know, like a real artist, and I pictured that title printed up on little cards and hanging above them."

"I don't think that's such a good idea."

"In a way, I don't either. Anyway, I'd have to hold it out here in the shop. Cold Rest isn't much for art exhibitions."

Gary reached in his shirt pocket and took out a pack of cigarettes.

"I thought you quit."

"I did." He lit one, took a long drag, staring off into the woods, and said, "I think we ought to go look for Emma."

"Where would we start?"

"You don't want her to come back here, do you?"

I said, "I miss her so much sometimes I can't breathe."

Gary watched me for a while. "Over at the yard, Neil, who runs that place?"

"Nowadays," I said, "Bree Cold and her brother Ambrose. He's kind of a half-wit, though. The Colds always ran it. Town wouldn't be here without the company. They came here from—well, hell, nobody knows where, but they started it up during the Depression, and people came from all over that couldn't get work anywhere else."

"What goes on there? What are y'all digging out of the ground all day?"

"What are you pushing papers round the office for?"

Gary finished his cigarette and lit another one off that. "I don't know," he said. "I got some ideas. I think it's time I cut my losses and hit the road, but there's something I haven't told you and Sarah."

"You don't owe us any explanations."

"That last book, though, it sort of tanked. They've been doing that for a while, actually."

"Well." I put down my paintbrush. I wondered if he was going to try to borrow some money; we didn't have anything to give him. "It's not all bad here. Sarah says at least in Cold Rest we can get at the edges of something miraculous." *The price of living is dying, Sarah had told me, and even when Cold Rest has swallowed up the last of you whole you know you've been in the presence of something divine.*

"Something miraculous," Gary said. "Is that how she sees it?"

*

Emma called us last night.

Her voice sounded so far away on the telephone. Sarah started crying. She asked Emma if she needed anything, if we could send her money, if there was anything at all she'd let us do. Emma said no. She just wanted to let us know she was all right.

"Baby, sooner or later you'll have to come home," Sarah said, but Emma had already hung up.

I couldn't sleep after that; I'd be dropping off and I'd think I heard her voice. Then a storm moved over us, thunder and lightning and wind to wake the dead. I got up and prowled around for a while, looking out the windows like I was waiting for something, and finally I braved the torrent of rain to make a sprint out to my workshop. I tried to work on a new piece. Sarah had stopped going out there at all. She said it upset her stomach to see the things I was making nowadays. She said she couldn't even look at them, that she had to look *around* them, because they just seemed like objects gone wrong somehow.

It occurred to me while I was out there hammering bits of bone I'd salvaged from carcasses of deer and dead birds—filthy work—that I could do the kind of thing a decent man would never do. I could leave. I could just disappear and put Cold Rest behind me. I could make the last twenty years of my life vanish just like that. Start anew. I was still young enough to have another family even.

At the same time I had a funny feeling I'd missed the chance to do anything like that, that whatever was set in motion couldn't be stopped any longer.

The Moon Will Look Strange

We have always known in Cold Rest that we were waiting on something. We didn't know what, or if we'd see it in our lifetimes, but without ever talking about it among ourselves we all knew we were preparing for something bigger than any of us could conceive.

There is not much of a social life in Cold Rest except among the teenagers. Sarah and I had never had any real friends. I wondered what kind of devices other people were constructing behind the walls of their homes. I wondered what kind of poems Sarah was writing that she wasn't showing to me.

*

Gary found me in my workshop just as dawn was breaking. The storm had blown over but the sky had a tattered look about.

"I got the truck all loaded," he said. "I'm taking off. Sure you don't want to join me?"

I said, "I don't think it would do me any good." And, "What about your headaches?"

His eyes, I realized with a shock, were bright with tears. "I tell you," he said. "I've been scared shitless all along it's a brain tumor. I think something's bad wrong. I just want to get somewhere bright and warm. Thinking of heading down to Tybee Island. Remember, when we were kids?"

Laughing like fools splashing into waves big as houses. Crab legs at the restaurant with the red and white checkered oilcloth where you threw the shells into a hole in the middle of the table. The one hundred and seventy-eight steps to the top of the old lighthouse and the rumors of pirate gold.

I had a couple of twenties on me, but he wouldn't take them. "I just want to sit on the beach and take it all in," he said. "I don't think I'll need that."

"For gas money, then," I said. It seemed important that I try to do something for him. I watched him leave, his taillights disappearing down the driveway, and then I turned back to my sculptures. In the gathering morning light they glowed and seemed to sing to me.

Sarah was fixing breakfast when I went in, pancakes and sausage. "Gary left," she said, not a question. I nodded anyway and helped myself to some coffee. The clock above the sink that played Westminster chimes on the hour struck, and went on striking, and both of us counting and trying to look like we weren't. Fifteen, sixteen, seventeen.

"Goodness, that was strange," Sarah said when it finished, with a nervous laugh.

I have never tasted a meal less than I did that breakfast.

I looked out the window toward my workshop, and I kept seeing things. Holes in my vision like Sarah describes when she gets one of her migraines, only my head felt fine. I think I said I better head on to work. Sarah looked anxious and said, Did I have to go?

The Moon Will Look Strange

Once I turned onto the main road through town I saw I might not get far. The storm had been worse up that way; tree limbs torn and blown into the road, pieces of asphalt chunked into rubble like there'd been an earthquake. It was still passable, barely, but I couldn't see any reason to pass. I turned around and headed back home.

Only now I'm here and Sarah's gone. I've called her name, and I've gone looking for her, and her cup of coffee is half-drunk and still on the table where she was sitting when I left. I tell myself she went on to work, too, but there's only one road into town and I didn't pass her on my way back. I don't dare look in the garage because I don't want to see her car there. I don't dare leave the house now, in fact, or even look out the windows.

It has gone blacker than night outside, although I believe it is about eleven in the morning; I cannot be sure because my watch has begun running in reverse and the clock is chiming weird hours at uncertain intervals. A little while ago there was a splitting sound, and I heard things scuttling and then swarming the sides of the house; it is only a matter of time now before what is out there gets in. We have always known there was something hidden in Cold Rest, something murmuring in a pitch not known to us, something waiting just outside our field of vision. We have obliged it with our reticent ways; we have nurtured it in our guarded, secret souls; we have made it potent with our lies; and now it is upon us all, all of us dreamers, whispering of promises we didn't mean to make, and cold as the stars.

Lynda E. Rucker

Different Angels

In the swelling, oppressive heat of a Georgia midday, Jolie came home. She choked on the red clay dust clouds billowing from beneath the wheels of the old Chevy that dropped her off a half-mile past the end of the paved road. They had picked her up walking on the Calhoun Falls highway headed out of town. Jolie could see the concerned faces of the snot-nosed kids with whom she'd shared the back seat pressing against the window, until the car dipped down a hill and out of sight. Her fingers were slick on the strap of the overnight-sized suitcase she carried, and she let it slip to the ground. Something rustled in the underbrush and she closed her eyes: snakes, maybe? Black racers, rattlers, moccasins, moving fast and striking swift before she had time to run?

She breathed in deep and smelled the honeysuckle twining there on the side of the road, and the mellow reek of cow shit in the pastures beyond, and the secretive stink of her own sweat. The smells were almost as good as a time machine. They took her back to that last summer of 1985. "The last summer" she'd called it then, too, even before she'd ever really believed she'd be leaving. She had spent it in cool church sanctuaries, wearing ugly pantyhose and uglier shoes, slipping out after Bible study to make out with the college bound boys. She imagined that something in those aloof intimacies might transfer that power of escape to her.

Even after the scholarship, her father said she wasn't going off anyplace where she was going to get ideas about being better than she was, better than all the rest of them. She called the place a shithole, a redneck, white-trash, low-class goddamn piece of shit town. Kind of town you wanted to raise your kids up in, the city elders said, while unbeknownst to them their kids were doing speedballs down at the river and humping one another with the frenzy of dogs in heat. Kind of place everyone talked about running far, far away from and no one ever did.

Those same kids grew up to be city elders themselves, and talked about what a good, God-fearing community they all resided in. So Jolie held out little hope for escape until that late August night when ashes fell through the air like they came from the sky, from heaven—if heaven could ever be so generous, so just. The firemen said her father's last careless cigarette had freed her; wherever her salvation had come from, Jolie had not believed until then that she would ever leave.

She picked her way up the clayey dirt road, here where the pine forests harvested by timber companies had grown back at last, round this bend where the heavy summer rains sent you sloughing off into the ditch if you weren't careful to drive real slow. Now over this hill and home again.

The house stood at the end of a stretch of gravel, a white clapboard front she'd never seen, rebuilt since the fire. A new porch, too. Her mouth was dry and the air filled with the sounds of beating wings and hissing tongues, as though the moment she set foot here again, they had awakened. As though ten long years had not passed for them at all. *Get thee behind me*, she told them.

As she trudged toward the house that was nothing like her memory, her sister LuAnn stepped out onto the porch, shading her eyes, and spotted her. LuAnn's mouth dropped open and she ran as fast as her short chubby legs could carry her. Her teeth were stained yellow and her hot tears washed Jolie's neck as she threw her arms around her. She smelled like coffee and cigarettes. Where had she been and how did she get out there, LuAnn wanted to know; she had been waiting by the phone all morning for her call. Jolie didn't answer any of her queries. She couldn't think of what to say, and couldn't imagine how to tell LuAnn just how badly she'd need her first moments out here to be alone ones.

"You didn't let somebody bring you out here, did you?" LuAnn asked. "Oh, honey, you did, didn't you! You ought not to have done that. You can't never tell about people nowadays." LuAnn had put on a fair amount of weight in the last decade and a half, but her face remained the same, small and sharp, ringed with frizzy curls.

"You ain't going away again, are you hon?" LuAnn went on. "You know you can stay here, long as you want." It was the invitation you extended to someone coming home in defeat, the last job lost, the apartment broken into, another man gone, the precarious life crumbled.

"I just got tired," Jolie said, and it was mostly true. Her grand escape had been the grandest thing in her life so far; peoples' lives in the cities up north were just as dead-end as anyone's back home. Up north was just one long endless waiting for something that never came. Up north was purgatory.

LuAnn stepped back and the sun behind her lit up her light-colored hair like a halo. Jolie squinted, still trying to study LuAnn's features, wondering if she might go blind in doing so. Would it truly be such a bad thing to sear her retinas useless? She could stand the lack of sight, as long as it truly left her in darkness and not gazing eternally at a bleached, white, shining light. She'd always heard heaven described as a great lit place, and thought there was nothing more horrific than a God who disallowed you your secret crevices, your hiding places. You'd be like an inmate sentenced to solitary confinement under a hellish burning bulb for all eternity.

"Let's get you something to eat," LuAnn said, hustling her up on the porch. Tears gleamed bright in her eyes. "I can't hardly believe you're standing right here in front of me. I used to say, Ray, the one thing I wish for before I die is that my sister—" Her mouth turned down now, ugly though she meant kind sentiment; her chin shook.

"It's all right," Jolie said, touching her uselessly on the back and shoulders. But she stopped short at the threshold. In her dreams she always returned home to a ruin, gutted throughout, when in truth only part of the house had burned. LuAnn had been long gone by the time of the fire, sharing an apartment with a girl in town; perhaps then she felt under no obligation to preserve any reminders of that fateful night. But it was not only the rebuilding which had altered the look of the place. She let LuAnn push her past the screen door into a living room where a cream-colored furniture set had replaced their parents' heavy old wood pieces. Jolie missed their weighty quality. That kind of furniture kept things anchored. Beyond, the kitchen, which had always hung heavy with stale cooking odors, was modernized beyond recognition. All the cabinets had been torn out and replaced with new ones; even the floor was retiled. Jolie ran one hand along a light beige countertop. Everything here was cool and distant, welcoming her with the disinterested air of duty.

"Beulah and them called earlier," LuAnn said. "They want to come over for dinner tonight and see you. I told them you might be wore out, I'd have to check with you first."

Jolie tried not to conjure any pictures of her aunt but they came anyway: a pinched, pious woman who'd probably been born old, though Jolie had seen pictures to the contrary. She dyed her hair a severe black above wrinkled skin, as if that fooled anyone, and had always made Jolie feel as if she smelled bad, or had snot smeared all over her face.

"I want to see the rest of the house," Jolie said. She realized she was desperate to see it, she wanted to touch all those surfaces again and stand in the middle of rooms and try to bring it all back again. "I want to see my old room."

LuAnn kept one hand on her back as she led her up the stairs, down the hallway. "I think if I don't keep touching you, you'll disappear," she said with a clipped nervous laugh, and she swung open the door of the room at the end of the hall. "I'm afraid we let your old room go all to seed, hon."

The Moon Will Look Strange

Jolie stepped past her into a shadowy stillness. Heavy blinds covered both windows. For a moment she imagined she saw the squares of her old posters still on the wall, and the rickety bookcases crammed full, but LuAnn flicked the light on and she saw she'd been mistaken. It had become a room of cast-offs, of ugly lamps, appliances that didn't work, boxes no one would ever unpack. Jolie let her breath out. It had never been a sanctuary for her. When she was a little girl, her mother and Aunt Beulah had come back from a shopping trip with a picture of Jesus for her to hang on the wall. Jesus was supposed to be floating in some cloudy heaven, His arms outstretched to welcome her and love radiating from him in great jagged halo-like bursts of yellow and orange. But Jolie wasn't fooled. She knew that what Beulah and her mother had told her was holy light was in fact the flames of hell, the flames she'd heard so much about. And if Jesus could be sent to burn in hell, then anyone could be. She was sure to be consumed by those same flames. Her mother told her to hang it on the wall so Jesus could watch over her all the time, but Jolie knew that was just so Jesus could spy on her and report back to God. And maybe God would let him come back up from hell.

"I am hungry after all," Jolie said, not wanting to be in the room any longer. She hoped that wasn't where Ray and LuAnn planned to put her up at night. She wouldn't be able to sleep, even with that picture long gone, even with the room all changed. She'd still be able to see those flames before her in the darkness, the coiling and hissing of the serpents Jesus had trained to do his bidding, the cool beatific smile promising her something she didn't yet understand.

*

LuAnn scooped up scrambled eggs and pieces of rubbery bacon onto plates for both of them, and set one in front of Jolie. "I know it's bad for you," she said, "but Ray's got high cholesterol and we don't never get to eat nothing like this. I'll make a stir-fry tonight, that all right with you?" She didn't wait for Jolie to answer, but went right on talking about neighbors, and people they'd gone to school with. Jolie remembered them only vaguely, as if she'd dreamed them, perhaps.

"You remember old Donny Spinks?" LuAnn said, and that was a name Jolie did know. Old Donny had lived in sin a few miles up the road from them with a woman maybe half Indian or Oriental, nobody knew so they just called her a half-breed. Even the church ladies refused to go out there to witness. Donny's land bordered on Jolie's granddaddy's field, a patch of dark woods leading to the junked yard and broken-down house where he lived. He had plenty of money, people said, even though he lived like a pauper there. When she was nine, old Donny had saved her from getting snakebit by the creek down the hill from his house, chopping off a rattler's head just before it struck at her. She had only seen him a few times before that, walking down the road or filling up his grocery cart at the Winn Dixie in town, where people gave him a wide berth. That day she'd followed him up into his backyard, a tangle of weeds grown up half as tall as Jolie and old tires rotting next to a half-gutted washer and dryer, a refrigerator, a sun-faded, rain-soaked couch with foam bursting out of the fabric. He had tried to get her to go inside and have a drink of water, but Jolie was not going to set foot inside that house. A woman's figure stood just on the other side of the screen, watching them. Jolie didn't ask to go to the bathroom, either, even though she was about to pee in her pants. Walking home that day, she'd stopped on the side of the road and squatted in the woods, letting the warm urine trickle out onto the leaves. Afterwards her panties felt moist and dirty.

"He died last year," LuAnn said. "Awful how it happened. I guess his daughter went out to see him—I didn't even know he had a daughter, did you? Anyway, he'd been dead a long time. Drank himself to death. They said the animals had got to him some. And his daughter, well, I guess she's just as crazy as he was, cause she waited a whole three days before she called anybody. She just set out there with his body, I guess. It must have stank to high heaven."

"God," Jolie said, and forked up some of the bacon and eggs. She chewed for a long time, but the food just stayed there, an unshrinking clot of grease and fat lingering in her mouth. She was embarrassed to think of seeing anyone she'd known. She who'd headed so proudly north without an inkling of the handicaps she toted with her, from the drawl that marked her as an ignorant redneck the moment she opened her mouth to that Jesus, burning in the flames, damned for all eternity and assuring her of her own fate, too. And she didn't want to see Beulah or her cousins, either, she didn't want to see anyone at all.

Lynda E. Rucker

She only wanted to be in the woods again, the way she'd been as a child, mapping the marshes and following the old sawmill roads and happening upon the bleached-white skulls of long-dead cows, their eye sockets huge and mortal and empty. She used to think she could find God out there. The preacher called that kind of thinking paganism, which was the next thing to worshipping the devil as far as he could see. At night Jolie dreamed of the devil, a huge brown reptilian creature reared up on powerful haunches, with a thick pointed tail. Hunched, as though he'd only recently learned to walk erect, his head was huge, vicious curved horns erupting on either side of it. In her dreams he tunneled up from someplace in the woods, and came up from a hole in the ground near where her mother used to plant jonquils in the spring. For months afterwards Jolie avoided that part of the yard after dark. The only place she really felt safe was the old barn in Granddaddy's pasture. "You stay away from there, Jolie," her father had told her. He said it was full of rusty nails and rats, and she could fall through a floorboard in the loft, or get bit by something and die of lockjaw. Jolie rarely defied her parents as a child, but she'd found that one private place irresistible.

"Ray's getting off his shift at the plant soon," LuAnn said, her gaze straying toward the clock on the oven. "I got to go pick him up, you want to come? He'll be tickled to death to finally meet you."

"I think I'll stay here and take a nap," Jolie said. She could hardly wait to see LuAnn backing her car up the driveway. Her breath came in short, tight, anticipating gasps; she was alone here at long last.

The Moon Will Look Strange

*

Her granddaddy's property could be reached by the road if you were willing to walk a couple of winding miles, but the shortcut was through the woods. Jolie's head pounded from thirst, and salty sweat dripped from her upper lip into her mouth. She slapped at a constant irritation of gnats and mosquitoes whining round her. The heat made breathing difficult.

She thought about snakes, poisonous snakes sunning themselves, the quick lash of a viper's tongue. The sky would fill with the sounds of their beating wings. She did not know if she would be strong enough to will them away. She pressed on.

The pond in the middle of Granddaddy's pasture had lost much of its water, and a brown ring of mud surrounded it now. The rowboat she'd been forbidden to play in as a child, even to sit in for fun, had vanished. The barn beyond shimmered like a mirage in the heat. At the opposite end of the field Donny Spinks' woods grew dark and tangled as she remembered them, no signs saying they were leased to the One Shot Hunting Club like most of the land around here, not even a Posted: No Trespassing warning. She wondered who claimed them now. Donny's daughter, she guessed, gone away to wherever she'd come from in the first place and letting the place run even wilder than before.

The barn had fallen into worse repair, the formerly padlocked doors unsecured and sagging on rusty hinges. Jolie pushed them apart. Inside, it smelled of abandonment and decay. When she was a kid she'd pulled loose boards apart at the back and slipped her skinny body through.

Birds rustled in the eaves above and sunlight spilled through splintered wood. While the stalls had in some cases collapsed entirely, the ladder to the loft still stood. Jolie gripped it with both hands and set a foot on the first rung, bouncing a little. It held firm.

The first few times she'd climbed the ladder had been scary ones. Once she'd made the mistake of looking down, and the earthen floor below her spun while she clung to the rungs, unable to move at all for a long time. Now Jolie lifted her other foot, and was suspended above the ground. She waited another moment, testing for the slightest indication of a *give* to the board, but felt nothing.

One foot up, one hand over. The next rung felt steady too. Again she waited before lifting the other foot and placing her full weight there.

You came back for this.

Halfway up, she stopped and looked down. The floor of the barn was very far away. She'd hurt herself badly if she fell. She didn't allow herself to look down again as she climbed. One rung did feel soft and rotted as the toe of her shoe pressed it, and she bypassed it, contorting her body to step up two rungs at once. And now, at last, the loft above.

Scattered sunlight lit patches of dusty boards. No one had used this as a real hayloft since her father was a child. She'd slept up here, and read enormous old books pilfered from her grandfather's library. And then, one long Indian summer when she was nine years old, it had been taken from her, her last

The Moon Will Look Strange

sanctuary, her last private spot. She'd been awakened by the noise of someone groaning, someone hurt in the barn. Peering through the opening, down past the ladder, she'd realized that the padlock was not secured; a space of light showed through the doors. She took the rungs swiftly. Heart pounding, she made her way down the row of empty stalls, sneakers scuffing on the hard-packed floor.

In the last stall on her right, a naked man moved atop a woman, making the groaning noise. Jolie's hand flew to cover her mouth and stifle the little noise that tried to escape. She had heard puzzling talk of *sex* around school, fourth graders whispering as though it were some forbidden country someone occasionally stole back from with a little more information. She'd never imagined it would look so absurd. A second later the woman opened her eyes and Jolie recognized her Aunt Beulah.

"*Wade*," Aunt Beulah said to the man grunting and heaving atop her, her eyes locked with Jolie's and that was when Jolie realized that was her father there with her aunt.

But he wouldn't stop; and Jolie stood like she was frozen, still staring at Aunt Beulah, Aunt Beulah still staring back, so long it seemed like just this side of forever. At last her father gave a final heave and was still.

"What the hell is wrong with you?" he snarled at Aunt Beulah, rolling off of her, and in the act of doing so caught sight of his daughter.

For a moment their eyes met, and Jolie had the horrible feeling that her father was going to try to say something to her, try to talk to her. She tried not to look at him at all, especially not below his waist where his *thing* dangled. It was enormous, and made her think of some sort of weapon. Her father opened his mouth, and Jolie broke into a run. She ran past him to the front of the barn and slammed the doors apart so hard that splinters tore into her palms.

Remembering, Jolie wished now she'd never climbed into the loft; she couldn't think how she'd ever get back down that rotted ladder. Now the sounds of fornicators in ecstasy rose up from below; or was it the groans and shrieks of the damned? The stench reached her nostrils a second later. She'd been staring out at the field, into the sunlight, and the brilliance of the day outside made it difficult for her to see the dark interior. But she knew what the smell was: old Donny Spinks, dead like LuAnn had told her in a pool of his own vomit.

And she couldn't stop remembering. That long-ago day she had run as fast as she could, across the field and into the woods, woods she didn't know like she knew the others because she'd been told to stay off other people's property, woods she could get lost in. Donny Spinks came upon her there, crying by the creek, the rattlesnake chittering inches from her as it poised to strike. Donny's axe came down right by Jolie's head and she started screaming, thinking he meant to kill her.

After he took her up in his yard, she saw how he'd combed his hair up in neat tufts so no one could see the horns sprouting there. He didn't look like the devil in her dream at all, not right at first, but Jolie knew better than to be fooled by appearances. She saw how the mark of the beast was woven in with the military tattoos across his arm, and she saw the flames reflected in his eyes. Was Jesus there too, trying to get out? She wasn't sure whose miracle had saved her. Did it matter anymore?

Twenty years later, maybe it did. A sob escaped her there in the loft, and Jolie took another step forward toward the smell. Another, and another—and before her now, a whole nest of dead snakes, ripe and rotting, their bodies swollen with maggots. The sob nearly turned into a giggle of relief before she realized that he had changed himself into something else, wasn't that what the devil did? Changing himself into a serpent, what did it matter one or many, live or dead? How else could snakes get up into a loft, if not through some divine or diabolical influence?

Jolie had tried to tell her mother what had happened in the loft. She had tried to tell her that very afternoon that she got home from Donny Spinks' house, and her mother had slapped her and called her a nasty, terrible little girl. She sent Jolie straight to her room, where the picture of Jesus waited. He was extending His arms out to her and begging her to save Him. As she stared at Him, she thought she saw the flesh on first His arms and then his face begin to blacken and pop. You see how it is, He told her as blisters on His face burst and oozed. Then His head narrowed and flattened, His eyes slid back until they were on either side of His head, and a long forked tongue snapped out at her. *You ssssee*, he hissed. *Are you going to help me?*

The snakes before her now were dead, not hissing, not speaking to her. Jolie stumbled backward from them, and the board with most of her weight on it gave way with a sickening crack.

One foot plunged through the rotted wood. She crashed to one knee, half of her body still on solid floor. She leaned backwards, palms down behind her, and scooted herself back. Her raw and bleeding leg she held out stiff before her.

Jolie began to breathe very deliberately. She would have to get back over to the ladder and down again, but the recklessness which had possessed her earlier had fled. She lay flat on her back, hoping to distribute her weight across the boards, then rolled over on her stomach and began to drag herself across the loft. The air, suffused with the reek of the dead things in the corner, bore down on her, hot and fetid.

When she reached the ladder, she looked at the nails and upper rungs and wondered that she'd made it to the top. She pulled on one of the nails holding the ladder secure and felt it give, bits of wood crumbling. She would set her weight on it, and the entire structure would collapse. The floor was too far away to jump. If she did not descend soon, the floor here could give way, too. She needed another miracle, a miracle like with the rattlesnakes, and the fire. Jolie was the only one who knew how the fire had really happened. It hadn't been her daddy's cigarette like the firemen had thought. She had looked out the window and seen them coming, a whole army of them, carrying torches as they flew across the sky, coming at last to bring her freedom from that place, just as Jesus had promised her when she was a child. They'd been terrible creatures, not at all like the pictures in her Bible, or hanging up in the Sunday

The Moon Will Look Strange

school rooms at church. Angels or demons, she wasn't sure: some vile combination of the two. Through the long terrible night that followed, of smoke-burned lungs and seared flesh and desperate attempts to contain the fire before it spread to the woods, Jesus came to her. He told her everything was okay; it was Him that woke her up and got her out of the house before the smoke choked her to death like it did her parents. He told her she was free now, but she had to run north and never look back. He and the devil had a lot still to work out, and she better go while she could.

Jolie dragged herself forward another few inches, hiking her shirt up and scraping her stomach on the rough boards. Her foot struck another soft patch of wood and punched through. Another sob rattled her breathing. Now she was too frightened to move forward at all. Things fouled quickly in this heat; her own body would ripen and burst just as the snakes had. "Oh, God," she said out loud, without thinking, and then, "Oh, Jesus," because she'd never thought much about God, but Jesus had always been there for her.

She didn't like having the dead things out of her sight. She was afraid to shift so that she could see them. She panted hard, the rotting-flesh smell turning her stomach, the fear clenching her insides up in knots. By the time anyone found her it would be too late. Already her stomach swelled, the maggots breeding inside her.

Jolie stretched her hands out and pulled on the ladder again. A piece of wood the size of her hand crumbled away, leaving the shaft of the rusted nail entirely exposed. And then she heard the terrible rushing in the air as they descended at last, the serpents with angels' wings. They disguised themselves that way so you couldn't tell who sent them, but Jolie was no longer fooled.

Her hand grabbed for the solid top rung of the ladder, wanting only to reassure herself of its remaining strength. The rung split in half as she grasped it, one piece tumbling the floor below. Jolie moaned. They were all around her now.

They lined up alongside her and folded their flat smooth heads in pious prayer, while their forked tongues slipped from their mouths and their snake bodies writhed in unseemly ecstasy. Jolie let them settle their feather-soft wings on her, run their tongues along the length of her body and back again. A gentle swell from their wings lifted her from where she lay, flat on her stomach, and she could see out the window at the front of the loft, see the drying pond glistening, and the fields golden in the noonday sun, and the cool dark of the woods beyond.

The Last Reel

"Wait a minute," Sophie said, "give me a clue, I know this one."

"If you know it, you don't need a clue, do you?" Kevin lit another cigarette and sank back against the seat.

She shot him a look. "Watch the road," he cautioned, and she reached over to punch him in the shoulder.

"Smartass," she said.

He sang softly, in a deep false bass. "Seven, seven, seven . . ."

"*The Magnificent Seven*," she finished for him. "I said give me a clue, not give it away."

"Well, if you didn't get the *Seven Samurai* reference what could I—"

Sophie hit the brakes. The car slewed to the right and skidded to a stop.

"That was the turn back there," she said. "Way to go, navigator."

"I know that one. Kiwi film about Black Death victims who time-travel to modern-day New Zealand. And there was a Buster Keaton flick with the same name. Either way, I am trouncing your ass!"

"That wasn't part of the game. Could you stop being a movie geek for five damn minutes?" Sophie asked rhetorically, dragging the gear stick into reverse.

"I'm a film critic. I know no other way."

"Well, next time we'll play some kind of—of *cooking* game or something and I will trounce your ass, as you so elegantly put it."

"A cooking game? Food geek."

"At least we eat well. You guys would live on popcorn and Junior Mints if it wasn't for people like me."

The missed turn was unsignposted and, he noted, not visible until you were upon it and saw the break in the trees and brush that grew right to the edge of the highway. He decided not to mount a self-defense at that particular moment.

"Great," Sophie murmured moments later as they bumped up the narrow gravel lane, rocks popping ominously against the underside of the car, branches scraping at the sides. "I wonder if the rental company has a 'back of beyond' clause absolving us from damages incurred in the actual middle of nowhere . . ."

She trailed off as they rounded a bend and the house was before them, all at once. It lurked in a clearing where all the grass had died and been dug up by the six dogs Sophie's Aunt Rose had kept. According to the animal control people they were all feral, and had to be destroyed.

The house itself was low and dark, all blank windows and weathered boards the color of old dishwater.

Kevin said, "It's haunted, right? I mean, it would have to be. Jesus, what a dump." He hated the way his voice went up at the end, losing control a little bit like the sight of the house had really shaken him. "Jesus," he said again.

"Well. It's not like we have to spend the night here or anything." Sophie was brisk, the way she always got when something made her uneasy.

"*House on Haunted Hill*," he said.

"What?"

"William Castle feature. Vincent Price offers ten thousand dollars to whoever will spend the entire night in a haunted house."

"Ah, but ten thousand dollars doesn't go nearly as far as it did back in those days, even if having Mr. Vincent Price do the offering makes it a little more attractive. Did they up the going price in the remake?"

"In the what?"

"The remake."

"Blasphemer!" he said.

"Race you!" she answered. She was out the door before he knew it, her sandals clattering on the steps when he was only halfway cross the yard.

"No fair," he said, "you tricked me." They were both laughing until she turned round to face the house, when it suddenly seemed rude to display too much levity as they prepared to survey the meager estate of poor deceased Aunt Rose.

*

Lynda E. Rucker

Sophie's key stuck in the front door, and for a moment he hoped it wouldn't work at all, but then the lock turned easily. The dark spilled out.

They crossed the threshold into a foyer smelling of mold, and stale with the heat of a hot September day. Just a few feet ahead he could make out monstrous shapes which were revealed, once Sophie touched the light switch, to be a coatrack bearing numerous heavy coats, and a hulking wardrobe. The hallway was short, a few steps across the worn grey carpet carrying him to the end.

Sophie had shown him photos late last night at her mother's condo back in Atlanta, the mutilated snapshots with sister Rose snipped from every one. It struck him as cruel and excessive, the way family interactions so often do to anyone on the outside, the story behind it all—for there always is one—too convoluted and painful to ever be properly recalled or recounted by the perceived injured party. *You have no idea what she did to me, you can't understand, you see she always.*

Already the estrangement made more sense, though, now that he'd seen the house. He tried to imagine two sisters more different than Sophie's bright, intimidating mother, vice-president of something-or-other at a big Atlanta bank, and this weird reclusive woman lost like a fairy tale witch in her spooky house in the woods. "Can you remember her at all?" he'd asked.

"Once," Sophie had told him; she'd been very young—she couldn't say for sure how young, but once, at some family gathering, maybe a funeral. "She scared me."

No, that wasn't right, her mother had insisted. Sophie and her Aunt Rose had never met. "I can't fathom any circumstance under which *that* would occur," her mother had told Kevin with a brittle laugh.

Sophie just shrugged. "She's lying. Aunt Rose taught me a weird little dance, like a jig or something, but then Mother made me stop doing it when she found out who I learned it from. So I used to do it in secret, in my bedroom." It was all, she said, that she did remember, and now scary Aunt Rose was dead and she was doing the responsible grown-up thing where her mother could not. *I'll go out there. I'll look the place over*, for crazy scary Aunt Rose had left the dump to Sophie in her will.

Sophie's mother had been opposed.

"I'm telling you, you don't even need to deal with it honey. You stay right where you are. I'll have people take care of it—get some appraisers out there, get the place sold, have the money deposited straight into your account."

The harder her mother pushed, the more Sophie's resolve grew to handle matters her own way. Kevin stayed silent and stayed out of it.

*

The doors to either side of them leading out of the foyer were closed. "Well," Sophie said, and reached for the one on her right. Kevin had a moment of uneasiness as she passed into a darkness that swallowed her up. "Good God." A dim light went on and he joined her just at the doorway of the kitchen, where the rancid smell of spoiled food hit him full on. "Will you look at that," Sophie said, and he did. All three windows—one over the sink, and two at the front of the house—were covered with cardboard and held in place with black duct tape.

The rest of the room was unremarkable, old but standard appliances, rough wooden cabinets. The refrigerator door stood open, the bulb burned out, and unidentifiable bundles—perhaps packages of meat—littered the floor before it, some of them leaking thin rivulets of dark fluid. Scattered across the counter, lumps that had presumably been fruit or vegetables were grey and furry.

"I've worked in kitchens that were *almost* this unsanitary," Sophie said, but neither one of them smiled.

He wanted to tell her to stop then, not to go into any more rooms ahead of him. She'd laugh at him, or get annoyed. *This place is creepy enough, don't freak me out.*

"Enough seen," she said, pinching her nose, backing out, pulling the door shut after them. "How I hate to say this, but maybe my mother was right."

The other door, now. Blackness, but this time he was prepared for it. In the second before Sophie found the switch he heard her finger scrabbling along the wall. It reminded him of something dried out and dead.

"*Well*," said Sophie, "what have we here?"

"Wow," he said, struck stupid.

Even without the contrast of the squalid kitchen, the suffocating opulence of the living room would have been striking. Oriental rugs covered every inch of wall space, including, presumably, the windows. His knowledge of old furniture was confined to an occasional stroll through an antique mall back in Seattle, idly wondering what would possess people to pay hundreds of dollars for old Coca-Cola merchandise. But even his unpracticed eye spotted some value in the chaos of clashing eras and continents. A Chinese lacquer cabinet was wedged against one wall, next to it a couple of heavy ornate chairs, and a sleek Art Deco lamp. A mostly clear path meandered through the clutter to the opposite door, but you still had to make yourself compact to get through.

Sophie had already done so, fighting her way past a rolltop desk and tugging at an unremarkable looking occasional table that blocked the next door. He had a passing irrational urge to beg her not to open it. Too late anyway, as miraculous afternoon sunshine fell across her path.

"Auntie's bedroom," she said as she stepped through the doorway, and he hurried to join her with a growing anxiety that the first two rooms had left in him, a sense of being lost, buried alive.

The unblocked windows helped him to breathe easier. "I wish you'd stop going ahead of me," he said. Auntie's bedroom was as neat and bare as a nun's cell. A single iron bed, white pillows, white coverlet pulled up tight. One wooden nightstand, empty save for an overflowing ashtray and a crumpled cigarette package. The cigarette butts were ringed with bright red lipstick. They reminded him of how badly he wanted to smoke, and he fumbled for his lighter before remembering he'd left his pack in the car. He crossed to one of the windows.

"I can't see our car," he said.

"Of course not. You're looking out the back of the house."

But that was nonsense. He ought to be seeing the driveway, and the ruined front yard, but there was only a stretch of bare ground and then a line of trees thickening into forest. He had a sense then that they moved, like curtains fluttering when something stirred on the other side.

"Look," Sophie said. She lifted a shoebox from the other side of the bed and set it on the night table. He saw her flinch and jump back. The back of her hand caught the ashtray, and it smashed to the floor.

"Shit!" Sophie yelled.

"Are you okay?"

"I thought a spider ran out of the box. What an idiot."

He came round the side of the bed and saw beads of blood welling up on her legs and sandaled feet where the shattered glass had pierced her skin. "I'm okay," she said, "it just scared me. There's probably Band Aids in the bathroom." She pushed past him and opened the last door. He caught sight of a heavy porcelain sink and a bathtub on feet, then Sophie said, "Ew" and he went in after her. Brown water sputtered from the faucet.

"It's just because it hasn't been turned on in a while," he said, "it'll clear in a few minutes."

"No Band-Aids," she said, "no medicine cabinet, nothing. Apparently Aunt Rose didn't even use soap. Doesn't matter. They're shallow." Working in a kitchen had left her inured to minor cuts and burns. "Let's see what's in the box."

Let's not, he wanted to say, but what came out when he followed her back to the bed was, "Three movies featuring a head-in-a-box. Name them."

"God," she said, "do you have to be so morbid? *Seven*." She lifted the lid.

"That's one," he said, so he wouldn't shout something stupid and hysterical like *Don't look inside!*

"It's filled with photographs," she said. "*Bring Me the Head of Alfredo Garcia*."

"That's head-in-a-bag, not head-in-a-box," he said desperately.

"Oh, for God's sake. Picky, aren't we?" Her voice changed. "That's weird."

"What?"

"I don't know how she got hold of these. It's all pictures of *me*."

*

So. What's the story with your mom and your Aunt Rose? he'd asked.

Mom always said she was a witch.

A witch . . . Like a Wicca-witch? New Agey, blessed be and white magic and all that? Like Teresa? Teresa was their neighbor back in Seattle.

No, I mean a bad old witch. Yeah, hard to believe, isn't it? It's the one subject guaranteed to make my rational mom completely irrational.

Then she said, *Also, something about my dad.*

Your dad . . . Sophie never talked about her

father.

When they were young. I don't know; they fought over him. He was Rose's boyfriend and Mom stole him, I think. I don't remember him at all.

She said it so cleanly, so matter-of-factly, that he couldn't believe she wasn't masking her pain.

He disappeared before I was three. Who are you when you're that young? You're not even through becoming a person yet—you don't have memories, even, just bright flashes of moments here and there, and what people remember for you, what they've told you so many times you start to think it belongs to you. He went away before I could have any part of him to myself.

*

"*Barton Fink*," she said. She was pulling out handfuls of photos and tossing them on the bed. Sophie as toddler in a birthday hat, Sophie grinning to expose missing teeth for an elementary school photo, Sophie wearing a strapless blue dress and holding hands with a skinny dark-haired boy at a high school dance.

"Check. That's two."

She grinned, waved snapshots at him in a less than menacing manner. "I'll show you the life of the mind!"

"You don't look a bit like John Goodman."

But she wasn't listening anymore. "What's this?"

He had a sinking feeling of inevitability, like the second or third time you watch a movie in which something terrible is going to happen, and even as you know it's coming, some part of you is hoping against hope that this time the film will magically find its path to a different fate. But this was not a movie, and it was nothing he'd seen before, so there was no reason for this sick feeling to engulf him when Sophie pulled a key out of the box.

"This is freaking me out," she said. "Where did she get all these pictures of me? And why'd she keep them?"

"Maybe your mom sent them to her." Families did weird stuff like that, mingling devotion and resentment, like his cousin Shelby who wouldn't speak to her dad but made her son write him a letter once a month.

"Sent a whole shoebox full of pictures?" she asked. He shrugged. "It looks like a door key," she went on. "I wonder . . . Kevin, do you have any idea how much that stuff in the other room is worth? What if this is the key to something even more valuable? Imagine if I came out of this with enough money to open my own restaurant?" Her eyes were shining when she looked at him. He wanted to take her hand and insist that they leave immediately, tell her that her mother was right and they should let other people deal with this.

Instead he said again, "This window ought to look out at the front yard. Why can't I see the car?"

"There's nothing *out* there." She was back at the doorway to the living room, tense and impatient. "There must be another room. Maybe she hung a rug over the doorway like she hid all the windows."

He lingered, not wanting to go back to the

stuffy closed-in part of the house. On a whim he tried one of the windows; it seemed important to have another route of escape besides the front door, and anyway he was noticing a heavy flowery scent hanging about, the kind of sickly sweetness used to disguise the odor of something foul. He took a deep breath, but could find no hint to the source of the rottenness underneath. It was not the same as the spoiled food in the kitchen; this was something earthier and more intense.

Fresh air would do him good. He tugged at the window, and it did not budge. It appeared to be painted shut.

When he walked back into the living room, Sophie had vanished. A woman stood with her back to him, shoulders rigid, black-haired, wearing Sophie's sweater. She turned and smiled at him, Sophie's smile, Sophie's eyes.

"Check out this funky wig," she said. "Wouldn't it be great for Halloween? What do you think my batty old aunt was doing with something like this?"

"Take it off," he pleaded, but he must not have sounded serious at all because she laughed and flounced past him. "Head in a box," she said. "Are you sure it's not *Bring me the Head of Alfredo Garcia*?"

"Of course I'm sure, it's my clue. I made it up," he said, but he could no longer remember what he'd had in mind for the third head-in-a-box film or why he'd started them on such a gruesome tack in the first place.

"Torso-in-a-box," she said. "*Boxing Helena*, ugh. You've got me. I need another clue." She had her back to him again, and her voice coming from the black-haired figure unnerved him. "Did I ever tell you what my Aunt Rose looked like?" she said. "She was beautiful once. Way more attractive than my mom. Mom got the brains, Rose got the beauty."

"How do you know that? That she was beautiful?"

"You know what?" She laughed. "I hid some pictures of her when I was little, before my mom got hold of all the rest and cut them to pieces. I still have them somewhere, I guess. When I was a kid and I'd get mad at my mom, I'd make up a story that an evil witch had taken her over, my real mom was actually Aunt Rose and that she and my dad were coming to rescue me. Isn't that stupid?"

"We should get going," he said. "There's nothing else out here, and it's a long drive back."

"That dance she taught me," Sophie said. "She called it the something reel. The witches' reel? Oh, I can't remember. Anyway, I just want to look around a little more. I want to see if we can find out what this key goes to."

He wanted to say that if it was truly concealing something so valuable, surely Aunt Rose would not make it so difficult to find and identify. Then again, Aunt Rose was at least a little bit crazy. Someone like Aunt Rose might think *I have to hide it, so no one finds it and steals it before she gets here.*

"I know," Sophie said. He followed her into the hallway, where she was tugging at the wardrobe.

"Be careful," he said, "you'll bring it down on yourself." He went forward to help her. "Take hold at the bottom here. We don't want to overbalance it." He had not noticed, when they first walked in, how much worse the smell was here. This place was sealed up so tightly, could the air go bad, like you heard about in caving collapses, mining disasters?

Between the two of them they heaved the wardrobe a couple of feet away from the wall. Sophie said, "Kevin, look. Come round on my side." She'd been right, after all; it had concealed a door, and she could twist the key in the lock and open the door just far enough to allow her to slip inside.

"Don't," he said, while she still stood on his side of the doorway, her hand on the knob.

She grinned at him. "Let's make a deal. You tell me the other head-in-a-box movie and I won't open it."

"I can't remember," he said. "I guess it was *Bring Me the Head*. Anyway, it wasn't even my turn just then."

"Not good enough," she said, and slipped into the darkness.

Long moments later she spoke. "I can't find a light switch. Maybe there's a string I can pull or something. Do you have your lighter?" She sounded as though she were speaking to him from the bottom of a well.

"It's in the car," he said. "Sophie, come out of there."

"Can't you just run out and get it for me? Come on, Kevin, five minutes and then we're gone."

The Moon Will Look Strange

He hesitated, then threw up his hands. "Fine." It was easier to get angry with her. He must have imagined the way the front door resisted him when he turned the knob; it was swollen from exposure, maybe, and that made it stick when he tugged at it. Then he was out on the porch again, where the day was still warm and sunny and their car waited just where he'd parked it. Halfway back to it he turned and searched for the bedroom windows he'd looked out from.

A movement on the roof caught his eye. Something scampered across the peak and out of his sight down the other side. Something blackened and low. *Just a squirrel.*

He snatched the lighter up from where he'd left it in the well between seats and sprinted back to the house. He called her name as he burst through the front door, and her voice came back to him, muffled.

"Oh, shit, Sophie, why'd you shut the door?" He slumped against the wardrobe, rattled the knob. "It's locked. Did you lock it?"

She sounded close—she must have been just on the other side of the door, but she might have been whispering against his ear. "There's nothing in here."

"Well, stay where you are. Don't go moving around in there when you can't see." But she was doing just that; he could hear her, thumping about. "Are you *dancing* in there?" *The something reel. The witches' reel.*

He'd once read somewhere that the best way to go about breaking down a door was to direct a blow near the lock.

"What are you *doing*?" Sophie said, as his foot smashed against it. His second kick splintered the wood; it was old and cheap and not made to keep anyone out. More than anything, he did not want to walk into that inky blackness. But he got the lighter out and struck at it once, twice, with the ball of his thumb. *Third time's the charm.*

As he stepped over the threshold, he was surprised at how much of the room it illuminated when he held it high over his head. He felt his shoulders sag, tension draining out of them as he asked himself what he'd been expecting to find in there; Sophie's father's head in a box, perhaps? She was right, it was a small, bare, perfectly square room, perhaps ten feet by ten.

Then he noticed the walls. He stepped forward, one, two paces. "Get up," he said. Sophie sat crosslegged in the middle of the room. The flame nipped at his thumb and he let the light go out.

He hoped that she had not seen what he had: every inch of wall space covered in thick black cursive writing or tattered pages torn from books, punctuated with photographs of Sophie. He thought that some of them had been hung upside down, perhaps defaced. He didn't want to look again to confirm it.

Sophie was silent. Then, "There's something painted on the floor here." She sounded different in the dark. They had been together for years; how could any nuance be unknown to him? He took a few more steps in. He felt swallowed by the blackness. "Bring the light over here."

The Moon Will Look Strange

His thumb was raw as he spun it against the wheel of the lighter. "Sophie," he said, and the little flame spewed; the room flickered once more in shades of grey. He squatted, and held the lighter down low and close between them. "Sophie, will you please take off that wig?"

She giggled, and that sounded wrong too. "If it's such a big deal to you," she said, and snatched it off, tossed it in a corner. He wished she hadn't done that, and almost asked her to pick it up. He hated the idea of it lying there like some furry dead thing, and he let the light go out once more.

"Your mother's going to get worried if we don't head back soon," he said.

"I wonder what's in the wardrobe?" she said.

"Your father's head?"

Silence again. Then, "That's not funny. Anyway, wouldn't be much left of it, would there?"

"I'm sorry. I was kidding. It was stupid." He could feel his shirt damp and stuck to his back, sweat trickling down his sides from his armpits. He became aware that his mouth hung open and he was breathing like he'd been running, heavy and ragged. "*Night Must Fall*."

"What?"

"*Night Must Fall*. That's the other movie with a head in it. I just remembered."

"Oh. I never heard of it."

"Albert Finney with an axe and a yen for decapitation."

"Oh," she said again. "That was kind of a cheat, then, if you knew I couldn't possibly get it." The boards creaked beneath her feet as she made her way over to him. He resisted the urge to recoil, but jumped anyway when she touched him. Her hand was icy through the cloth of his shirt, her fingernails sharp and hard. "It's so dark in here. Like there never was any light." Her breath was on his cheek, warm and moist and stale-smelling. "You know?" she said, and then she pressed against him and fixed her mouth on his. Her tongue invaded, prying his lips apart.

He stumbled back away from her. "We have to go."

She coughed, a phlegmy sound like she was a longtime smoker. "You're right," she said. "There's nothing here anyway."

He was relieved when she pushed past him and continued down the hall. The wig had left her hair matted and stuck to the crown of her head. When she opened the front door and he saw how the light had changed he realized how much later it was than he'd thought. She commented that it seemed to be growing dark so early these days, it was hard to believe that it wasn't yet fall.

"Sophie, those cuts look terrible," he said, noticing her legs. They'd gone dry and puckered looking, like tiny gaping mouths. But she was already crawling in on the passenger side, and didn't seem to hear him.

The engine failed to turn over the first time, then again and again, and sweat was dripping into his eyes. Sophie sat placid beside him, unmoved by the useless grinding of the motor.

"What's the number for Triple A?" he said. "Where's your phone?"

"It's dead. I forgot to recharge it last night." She went on, "It's not such a bad place, really. I bet we could do something with it."

"I forgot my lighter," he said.

"What?"

"Nothing," he said, already willing to forget that for a split second he'd thought of sending her back inside on the pretense of fetching something, then driving away—no, running away, a mile or more back up to the highway where he'd flag down a car. It wasn't Sophie that stopped him—rather, the certainty that he might run as far as he could and would never find the highway, because it would no longer be there.

"Poor thing," she said, "you must be tired. You probably shouldn't drive anyway. There's a bed inside, you know, if you need to rest."

He steadied his foot on the accelerator. He would feel better if only he would look at her, and she'd laugh, propose some calm and sensible plan for getting them out of this predicament. Someone will stop for us up on the highway, she'd say in a moment, out here in the country people still help you like that. But he could not do it. He found that a sort of numbness had taken him, rather than grief or any sense of loss, and he kept turning the key and pressing the gas long after it produced only a series of dry dead clicks, and still he could not bring himself to look into her eyes.

Lynda E. Rucker

ACKNOWLEDGMENTS

This book would not exist if not for the editors who encouraged me by buying my work, particularly early on, and in that vein, I have to extend particular thanks to Andy Cox of TTA Press, who bought my first two published stories — both reprinted here — and has continued to encourage me and publish my writing in the 14(!) years since "Different Angels" first appeared in the pages of the gone-but-never-forgotten *The Third Alternative*. Most of the stories in this book appeared there or in its successor, *Black Static*. Similarly, Stephen Jones bought my third published story, "No More A-Roving," for my first appearance in *The Mammoth Book of Best New Horror*, and he, too, has continued to encourage me and publish my writing in the years since. I can sincerely say that without Andy Cox and Stephen Jones, I would not have the writing career that I do today.

In fact, I took several years off from that writing career, and were it not for Michael Kelly asking me for a story for an anthology he was working on, I might have put off returning to it forever, so thanks go to him as well. In the end that story, "The Moon Will Look Strange," ended up at *Black Static* instead (through no fault or rejection of Mike's, I hasten to add!), but I have always sort of thought of it as

The Moon Will Look Strange

Mike's story.

Thanks go out to the other editors who published or reprinted or podcast the stories in this book as well: David Longhorn of *Supernatural Tales*, Mick Sims and Len Maynard, Paula Guran, Shawn Garrett, and Pete Bullock. When I was writing stories that didn't seem to fit anywhere or get much attention, each one of them gave me reason to keep going.

Jeanne Cavelos of the Odyssey Writing Workshop gave me my first taste of what it might feel like to be a "real writer"; Derek Hill was the first audience for all of these stories and encouraged me to keep writing them even when I felt like giving up. My parents, Carolyn Nance Rucker and the late Guy Rucker, Jr. believed in me from the moment I first picked up a pencil and begin writing (the two things occurred pretty much simultaneously), suffered through the reading of reams of juvenilia, and kept their weird, ambitious daughter supplied with typewriters, paper, books and books on writing and books of horror stories.

Finally, thanks go to Steve Rasnic Tem, a writer I have admired for decades for taking the time to read these stories and write a lovely introduction, and to my editor, Johnny Mains, who displayed uncommon degrees of persistence, patience, and painstakingness to put this collection together.

Lynda E. Rucker

Lynda E. Rucker

Karōshi Books is run by the editor of Salt Publishing's *Best British Horror* series, Johnny Mains, Peter Mark May, the owner of Hersham Horror Books, and Cathy Hurren, a production editor at Unbound Books.

KARŌSHI
BOOKS

The Moon Will Look Strange

Printed in Great
Britain
by Amazon